No words _____ ___ nd Callahan when _____ ___ under the rippling surface of the roiled water. As one man, they drummed their boot heels against their horses' flanks and reined the animals into the stream. By this time the water's surface was covered with small bursts of bubbles raised by the thrashing legs of the horse Meg had been riding. . . .

At almost the same moment both Longarm and Callahan saw Meg's head rise from one of the bubble-blotched stretches of the river . . . and her arms were splashing as she fought the dragging water. The men tugged at the reins of their mounts, but the animals did not respond as they would have if they'd been on solid ground.

"Get downriver from her," Longarm called to Callahan. "I'll try to make it to her from here."

* * *

SPECIAL PREVIEW

Turn to the back of this book for an exciting look at a new epic trilogy . . .

Northwest Destiny

. . . the sprawling saga of brotherhood, pride, and rage on the American frontier.

DON'T MISS THESE
ALL-ACTION WESTERN SERIES
FROM THE BERKLEY PUBLISHING GROUP

THE GUNSMITH by J. R. Roberts
Clint Adams was a legend among lawmen, outlaws, and ladies. They called him . . . the Gunsmith.

LONGARM by Tabor Evans
The popular long-running series about U.S. Deputy Marshal Long—his life, his loves, his fight for justice.

LONE STAR by Wesley Ellis
The blazing adventures of Jessica Starbuck and the martial arts master, Ki. Over eight million copies in print.

SLOCUM by Jake Logan
Today's longest-running action western. John Slocum rides a deadly trail of hot blood and cold steel.

TABOR EVANS

LONGARM

AND THE REBEL BRAND

JOVE BOOKS, NEW YORK

LONGARM AND THE REBEL BRAND

A Jove Book / published by arrangement with
the author

PRINTING HISTORY
Jove edition / September 1992

ISBN: 0-515-10929-0

Jove Books are published by The Berkley Publishing Group,
200 Madison Avenue, New York, New York 10016.
The name "JOVE" and the "J" logo
are trademarks belonging to Jove Publications, Inc.

AND THE
REBEL BRAND

Chapter 1

A streak of red muzzle blast cut the night's almost total blackness, and before the sudden flash had faded the sharp bark of a rifle-shot broke the silence. Even though Longarm and Billy Vail saw the red gash and knew that a good span of distance separated them from the gun-wielder, the shot had sounded as though it was within inches of their ears. They hunched down even lower in the narrow little arroyo where they'd taken cover.

When the escaped murderer they were following had let off his first shot several minutes earlier, they'd dropped to the ground in the narrow confines of the deep gully. That first rifle slug had missed by a wide margin, sending chips of stone from the solid rock above their heads, as had the bullet just fired by the man they were after.

Neither Longarm nor Vail wasted a cartridge by returning the rifle fire. Vail's voice was calm, as though he was commenting on the weather, when he remarked, "Well, that's two more rounds the damned fool's wasted."

Longarm's voice was equally casual when he replied to Vail. "Billy, I'd reckon the smartest thing we've done so

1

far was listening carefully to that conductor on the train. I guess you recall what he told us."

"Sure. He said that the old Henry rifle Pete Gorman stole from the baggage coach hasn't got but a five-round magazine, and the only shells for it they had on board the train were in the gun."

"And Gorman wasted one of them first off, right after we began chasing him," Longarm went on. "Those two he just triggered makes three. All we got to do now is tease him into letting off two more shots, and I figure it'll be safe for us to close in on him."

"Likely you're right," Vail agreed. "But when we do close in, let's be sure he's let off both of those rounds. Daylight or dark, that damn Gorman can move slicker than any eel I ever ran across, and he's got more tricks up his sleeve than both of us can count."

"Come to think of it, maybe the dark's as much of a friend to us as it is to Gorman."

"You mean even if we can't see him till we're right on top of him. It works the other way too?"

"Stands to reason, Billy. If we can't see him, Gorman can't see us closing in on him."

"Let's be grateful for small favors then."

"Sure. But come to think of it, I don't figure he'll stay where he is very long," Longarm said. "If he's got enough gumption to save his last two shells, he's likely smart enough to move away without making a lot of noise, which means we better close in on him now, just as fast as we can move."

"Then you say which way you want to go, Long. I'll take the other direction."

"It don't make no never-mind to me, Billy. Let's just turn around back-to-back and start moving."

Longarm did not need to say anything more. Vail nodded, his face a ghostly shimmering patch against the night's blackness. He climbed up out of the gully and turned to begin inching along the base of the massive solid rock formation, while Longarm followed behind him and then moved in the opposite direction. After they'd each taken a step or two neither man could see the other in the dense darkness.

Longarm advanced slowly, lowering his feet carefully to the coarse ground to make the smallest sounds possible. After he'd taken three or four short steps he could no longer hear Vail's muffled footsteps.

Above his head the huge towering mass of granite blotted out the stars behind its sharply slanting top, and the curve in its formation at ground level grew tighter as its size diminished. It also took on a more pronounced inward slope toward its base with each careful step Longarm took.

Sooner than he'd expected, Longarm passed the point where the curve in the huge mass of granite hid the terrain beyond. He could see only an arm's length ahead through the veil of night's blackness, and when the ground started to slant sharply downward his boot soles began to slip a bit with each step he took on the coarse hard-baked soil.

Longarm tried to hold himself erect by leaning forward against the rock face. At the spot he'd reached, the surface of the big stone formation was as smoothly slick as glass, and had no cracks or protrusions that would have given him something to grip. Pressing his palm against the stone, he tried to cup his palm and fingers to form a makeshift handhold, but his effort was useless.

He tried again. Even when he summoned all his considerable strength to make the effort, his hand still slid along the glassy, slippery surface of the weather-polished stone. Though he braced his feet and leaned against the rock face, Longarm could not prevent his feet from skidding on the loose gravel underfoot. He glanced at the down-stretch, an

3

expanse of loose stones that somewhat covered the unstable soil.

"Old son," he muttered against his clenched teeth, "if you ain't in a jam now you never will be. Looks like what you got to do if you want to get down where you're heading for, is put the big pot in the little pot whether it'll fit or not."

Now Longarm abandoned thought in favor of action. He gripped the rifle stock firmly in his left hand and stretched his right to press flatly against the smooth surface of the towering granite formation. He advanced one of his booted feet cautiously and leaned forward while he rotated the advanced foot in a small circle, trying to find a solid stretch of earth where he could put it down.

Even while he was just beginning to lean away Longarm felt his hand slipping along the slick surface of the huge granite slab. At that moment he realized that the downward slope of the hard earth beside the towering stone was much steeper than he'd anticipated. He tried to rear back and bring his body erect, but gravity's pull defeated him and he began plunging downward.

When Longarm started falling he instinctively tightened his grip on his rifle. He clung to it as his downward lean dragged him into what became a tumbling, rolling plunge. Now and then the flailing butt of his rifle banged into one of his legs, or clattered against the surface of the rock, but the stretch of steep slanting ground was mercifully short.

Longarm felt the sharpness of the incline moderating to a gentle slope, and though his fall had seemed as though it would never end, only a few moments passed before the plunge ended, leaving him lying prone but only slightly bruised on a stretch of high grass.

For a moment Longarm relaxed. He'd retained his grip on the throat of his rifle, and now he used it as a lever to pull himself to his feet. His first move was to drop his free hand to the butt of his holstered Colt to make sure the weapon had not been lost during his tumble.

While Longarm was still fingering the butt of his Colt after finding it safely in its holster, Vail's voice broke the silence that had followed the sounds of Longarm's unexpected downward slide.

"Are you all right, Long?" he asked.

"Righter'n I've been a lot of times before now," Longarm answered as he saw Vail's shadowy figure taking form through the darkness. Then, as the chief marshal reached his side and stopped, Longarm went on. "I sure hope that path you took was easier than the one I got caught on."

"It was steep, but it didn't give me any trouble," Vail replied. "But from what I heard you might've been a steer sliding down the wall of an arroyo."

"That's pretty much the way I felt for a few minutes, Billy. But I didn't break nothing nor even get more'n a bump or two. Now all we got to do is pick up Gorman's trail again and see if we can catch up with him."

"Dark as it is with the moon gone, we'll be bucking long odds," Vail replied. "But unless I'm mistaken, we're not the only ones to pass this way. Even in the dark I could see a pretty well-marked trail running along at the base of that big boulder we came around."

"Then all we've got to do is head back to where you were, and we'll be able to pick it up."

Vail nodded. "Remember, this stretch of country used to be Pete Gorman's stomping ground. I don't wonder but what he knew just about where to make his move when he jumped off the train."

"Let's go after him then. The longer we stand here, the further he'll be getting ahead of us."

Without wasting more words, they began moving side by side along the base of the big granite formation. Their

5

walk had lasted only a few minutes when Longarm raised his arm and stopped their forward progress.

"What's wrong?" Vail asked. "I haven't heard anything or seen anything we need to stop for."

Without replying, Longarm pointed to a bright glint on the coarse soil just ahead of them. Vail switched his eyes in the direction Longarm's finger was indicating.

"Unless I'm mistaken, that's shell brass," Vail said.

"That's what I make it out to be, Billy. Fresh brass too. If it'd been there long enough to color down, I never would've spotted it."

By this time, Longarm and Vail had reached the shell case. Longarm reached down to pick it up and hold it out for Vail to inspect.

"That's got to be out of the old Henry rifle Gorman stole," Vail said. "It's the right caliber. There's not all that many guns takes a fifty-seventy slug."

"I make it out to be the same," Longarm agreed. "And that gun'll send a slug two miles without batting an eyelash."

"We'd better see Gorman before he sees us then," Vail warned. "Him having enough gumption to save his last two shells means that he's one of the few smart outlaws."

"Why, we've known that a long time, Billy, but all we need to do is be a little bit smarter than he is."

"That's why my money's on you. I've seen you do a lot of tracking, and I can read trail-sign almost as easy as you can. We're close enough to pick up his trail and we both know enough to stay on it."

"Well, now," Longarm observed, "even if this is a stretch of country I don't know real good, from what little I've seen of it, there's not a lot of places where a man can find cover."

"You've called the turn on that," Vail said. "How long has it been since you worked a case in these parts?"

"Maybe two or three years, Billy. I don't rightly recollect. But I've been over it enough times to know how tricky it is. I recall going up a couple of blind coulees when I was after one or another of the outlaws that hole up here."

"I'd say we're a lot better off right now than we were when we started out from the train," Vail observed. "And since we've started to talking about it, I remember it wasn't any too far from these rocky hills that Gorman killed poor old Frank Corley. Frank was a fine lawman, but he just didn't hang up his gunbelt soon enough."

Longarm thought for a moment. "If Gorman really knows these parts he might just have a hidey-hole someplace close by. Don't that make sense?"

"I'd say it does," Vail agreed. "But right now let's give him a little more bait to nibble at."

While he spoke Vail was bending down to pick up another shard of rock. He lofted it into the impenetrable darkness ahead of them. When they heard the thud of its landing, both he and Longarm listened for a repetition of the shot that had greeted the first stone Vail had thrown, right after they'd begun chasing the escaped outlaw. A minute ticked by after the rock had grated when it dropped onto the stony soil, and they waited another minute after that, but this time no shot was fired in response to the clumsy missile. Longarm was the first to break the silence they'd held while listening.

"My guess is, he's moved," he said.

"Oh, I'm sure he has," Vail replied. "But we'd have to be up to our belly buttons in luck if we picked up his trail on a night as dark as this one is."

"I grant you that, Billy. And the dirt's baked hard enough so there ain't much of a chance he's left the kind of trail we'd be able to see even in the daytime. But I'd say that if we do a lot of zigging and zagging we oughta run across some kinda sign he's left."

"There's bound to be some soft spots on this damn hard ground. Between the two of us, we just might pick up a track or two."

"I'd be one to bet we can," Longarm said. "Especially since we know where Gorman started from. And the way I figure, we owe enough to poor old Frank Corley for us to keep on the tracks of the man that killed him."

"What you said is just about what I've been thinking," Vail said soberly. "Frank was as good a deputy as a man in my position could ask for."

"He sure did come through for me a couple of times, when we were working a case together. I reckon I owe him about as much as you do."

"Let's cover as much ground as we can as soon as there's light to see by then. We know that Gorman's short on ammunition. All we'd need to do is trick him into letting off those last two rounds he's got in that rifle he stole. Then he wouldn't have any choice but to give over."

"Not that he would, even if we gave him the chance to," Longarm observed. "But you're the boss, Billy. And if we ain't going to move from here till it's light enough to see what's ahead of us, we might as well catch up on our sleep."

"I'm as ready to do that as you are," Vail agreed. "The first one who wakes up when daylight gets here can rouse the other one, and we'll get started."

Longarm and Vail woke up at almost the same moment. They said nothing, but sat up and began scanning their position. Though the sky in the west was still dark, daylight shone from the opposite horizon, a pale light that promised the beginning of sunrise within a few more minutes. The expanse of bare rock-strewn ground that was visible below the high ledge where they'd bedded down gave little promise of holding footprints.

"This ain't the kind of a place I'd pick out to do any tracking in," Longarm observed. "But it's what we got."

"And we'll just have to make the best of it," Vail told him. "So let's get up and see what we can find."

For the first few seconds after getting on their feet both Longarm and Vail moved gingerly, shaking off the stiffness that always follows a night spent sleeping on bare hard ground. They took short careful steps, grimacing at the small twinges that followed any sudden movement. At much the same time as they realized that they were limbered up enough to move, both men thought of breakfast. They exchanged glances, and Vail shook his head.

"I don't carry grub in my pockets any more than you do," he told Longarm. "And we sure didn't have any idea we'd be jumping off that train. If I'd thought we'd be leaving it, I'd've bought an apple or something from the butcher boy when he came through the coach with his goodie-basket."

"Why, we've made out before when we didn't have a bite of grub, Billy," Longarm said. "And we'll likely pass a farm someplace along the way where we can buy what we need."

Longarm and Vail started moving. Longarm left for Vail the job of studying the terrain ahead, and concentrated on watching for the tracks left by their quarry along the rim of the steep bluff, and looking for a place where they could descend. They found it after a few minutes of walking, a narrow trail that showed evidence of being used often. The trail went through a wide fissure in the high stone escarpment and wound through a dense stand of head-high mesquite.

When Longarm and Vail emerged from the thick brush they saw that the trail forked into three separate paths. One branch led to the right and another ran leftward, both holding close to the heavy mesquite patch. The middle branch led away from the tall cliff and vanished in the distance beyond a sprawling stand of small saplings. Above the tops of the young trees a faint thread of smoke was visible, though its source was still hidden behind the trees and the rising grade of the saucerlike depression.

"Farmhouse, wouldn't you say?" Vail asked.

"Bound to be," Longarm agreed. "And the faster we walk the sooner we'll get to it. I don't mind telling you, Billy, it's been so long since we've had anything to eat that my belly thinks my throat's been cut."

"You can't be much hungrier than I am," Vail replied. "And the only place we're going to find any food is where people are. Let's get moving toward that smoke."

They started along the middle trail toward the wavering line of smoke. The path was an easy one, and the stiffness that remained from their night on the bare ground faded quickly. Even before they reached the immature trees the thin thread of smoke that had been their guide faded and vanished, but they'd established a course now, and kept to it in spite of the small growls and rumbles from their protesting stomachs.

Breaking through the stand of saplings, Longarm and Vail stopped at its edge and peered at the terrain ahead. Beyond a wide expanse of freshly plowed ground they saw a small house and a huge barn. There was no one around either of the buildings, no animals in the modestly sized fenced area that adjoined the barn, but the shimmer of heat that rose from the smokeless chimney of the dwelling told its own story.

"Now's the time to watch our p's and q's," Vail said as they stopped at the edge of the brush line. "It's dollars to doughnuts that Gorman's either in the house or the barn.

My guess is that he'll be ready to use up those last shells in his rifle the minute we get close on that bare stretch of ground."

"Oh, I wouldn't argue that," Longarm said. "And it'd take a long time to circle around all this plowed-up land to get at him from behind. But if we keep in the cover of these bushes we just came through we can split up and head for the house from different sides. That way we'll have a better chance to get there with our skins whole."

"You've hit the mark square," Vail said. "Let's do it that way."

Separating, they started moving in opposite directions, Vail going to the right and Longarm to the left, keeping in the shelter of the underbrush.

Chapter 2

Neither Longarm nor Vail spoke or paused after they moved apart and started for the farmhouse and barn, though both took occasional over-the-shoulder glances to make sure they would know when to turn in order to start together toward the buildings. Longarm broke cover first. He stepped out of the brush onto the bare expanse of plowed land, ready to drop flat at the first sign of motion from the dwelling or the barn.

When no shot came from the farmhouse Longarm looked back in the direction Vail had taken. Vail had already turned to head for the two structures, and Longarm was starting to turn away and continue his advance when he saw his chief drop flat on the ground.

At almost the same moment the crack of a rifle from the direction of the big barn reached his ears and Longarm followed Vail's example. As he raised his head to peer at the buildings ahead he now saw the thin yellow wispy vapor of gunsmoke rising in a small plume trickling above the barn from the half-door of a horse stall, the muzzle of a rifle disappearing inside.

"Looks like we got Gorman pinned down, Billy," he called.

"Not much doubt about that," Vail replied. "And we're in better shape than he is, because all he's got now is one more chance at us before he's a sitting duck!"

"I've just got a mind to knock that sitting duck off his perch," Longarm called. "But these Colts ain't got the range to do it as far away as we are. You cover me and I'll make a run for that barn."

"Wait a minute!" Vail shouted. "No use in you—" He broke off as Longarm propelled himself to his feet and began running in a patternless zigzag toward the barn.

As Longarm raced for his goal, Vail began running also. However, Longarm had gotten a head start. He was within pistol-shot range of the barn before Vail could come close to him or to their target.

In spite of Longarm's helter-skelter advance he'd never taken his eyes off the stall door where Gorman's shot had come from. He saw the muzzle of the old Henry rifle as it was being pushed out of the half-door of the barn. Beyond the muzzle of the weapon he could also glimpse the shadowy outline of the outlaw's figure.

Longarm fired while still running, his shot followed by what might have been an echo as Vail also fired. Gorman had the rifle leveled, but in the instant before he triggered off the last round remaining in the Henry's magazine, Longarm's lead reached him. The outlaw was reeling backward as he sagged and dropped, the lead slug from the big-bore rifle tearing a hole in the roof of the barn as it sailed into empty space.

Both Longarm and Vail were close enough now to see Gorman crumpling. Neither of them broke stride, but as the outlaw's head disappeared below the bottom of the half-door they ran at a slower pace. Vail reached the barn door first and peered inside, then turned around and waved to Longarm, flicking his hand in a signal that now it was safe. Longarm walked the short distance left between him and the chief marshal. He stopped beside Vail and joined him in looking at the corpse of the fugitive outlaw.

"He don't look no prettier dead than he did alive," Longarm commented.

"No," Vail agreed. "One of us sure got in the shot that finished the story. Now maybe we'd better find the folks that live here and let them know what this ruckus was all about."

"What I got in mind is doing a little bit more than telling 'em, Billy," Longarm replied. "What I need right about now is to sit down at a table and put away some breakfast."

"I don't imagine that'll be too hard to do," Vail told him, "farm folks being what they are. And we'll need to put away a good one, because we've still got some work to do."

"If I take that rightly, Billy, you aim for us to tote that dead outlaw back to the railroad tracks?"

"Dead or alive, we've got to turn him in. We'll flag the first train that comes along."

"Oh, sure," Longarm agreed. "But it's more'n just a step or two back to them railroad tracks, and most of it's uphill. I aim to get breakfast inside me before we take on that job."

"Oh, I'm on your side in needing some breakfast first," Vail answered. "Tell you what. As soon as we've finished we'll ask this farmer if he's got a horse and wagon that we can use to cart Gorman's body to the nearest stop on the railroad. Then we'll get rid of the body and get on the first train that comes along. I've got to hightail it back to Denver, because that's where I ought to be right this

15

minute, looking after the business Uncle Sam pays me to take care of."

"I'd sorta looked for you to say something like that," Longarm replied. "It ain't all that much of a surprise. And you know that I ain't one to . . ." He broke off and turned to look around when the sound of excited voices came from the direction of the house.

"I'd imagine that's the farm folks coming to see what's happened," Vail said.

"Likely," Longarm agreed. "When they didn't hear any more shooting, they figured it'd be all right for them to come find out what was going on."

"Well, it's their barn, so they've sure got a right to know what we're aiming to do."

A man and woman appeared around the corner of the barn. The man wore overalls bleached almost white from the sun and the washtub; the woman had on a dress mended so many times that it gave the appearance of being part of a patchwork quilt.

Vail took out the leather folder that held his badge and flipped it open for them to look at as he said, "We're United States marshals, folks. I'm Chief Marshal Vail, this man with me's Deputy Marshal Long. Now, in case you're wondering about the shooting you just heard, it was us. We've been chasing an escaped prisoner. Did you know that the man hiding in your barn was a prisoner who got away from us?"

"We couldn't help knowing, Marshal Vail, seeing as he kept that gun of his pointed at us a good part of last night and a while this morning," the man answered. "But then he seen you fellows on the way here. He'd asked if we had any horses on the place, and I had to tell him we did."

"That's when he left the house and run out here," the

16

woman said when the man stopped for breath. "And once he'd left, me and Delbert looked out and seen you men coming this way."

"He didn't hurt either one of you, though?" Longarm asked.

"All he done was he made us put him up in our house last night and feed him supper then and breakfast this morning," the man said. "He didn't hurt us none, but I don't mind telling you he sure give us a bad scare."

"He kept looking at me like—well, like he was wanting to have his way with me," the woman volunteered. "But I put what I had left in a vial of laudanum in his coffee when I give him his supper, and he had all the trouble he could handle just trying to keep awake and keep his gun pointed at us."

"You've been up all night then?" Longarm asked.

"Most of it," the man replied. "Ma was just fixing to give him his breakfast when he looked out and seen you two men coming up towards the house. Then he cut a shuck for the barn."

"You're sure he saw us?" Vail asked.

"Oh, he saw you, all right, because we looked out the window ourselves and you two was the first thing that caught our eyes. I figured out that you was likely to be lawmen, so I told Ma that if you was it was your job to corral him, and we better stay in the house and keep outa your way."

"Which was the smartest thing you could do," Vail told him. "But now I've got a favor to ask of you. If you've got a horse and wagon you can spare for a while, Marshal Long and me will take that outlaw's body to the closest railroad stop so you'll be rid of it. Of course, we'll see that you get your horse and wagon back, along with a government voucher to pay for letting us use them."

"Well, I don't see that we oughta get paid for letting you borrow our rig, Marshal Vail," the man said. "Voucher or no voucher, you're welcome to the use of it."

"And you're welcome to have a bite of breakfast too," the woman said. "Just in case you're hungry."

"Now, that's an invite we couldn't say no to," Longarm said before Vail had a chance to speak. Turning quickly to Vail, he smiled. "Don't you figure the same way, Billy?"

"I sure do," Vail answered. "And now that we're all agreed on what's what, I'm ready to sit down for a bite with these fine folks before we start out."

Trailing behind him the scent of the lotion that the barber had rubbed into his freshly shaven cheeks only a short time earlier, Longarm entered the chief marshal's Denver headquarters. He exchanged nods with the pink-cheeked young clerk as he crossed the outer office and glanced at the door to Vail's private room. It was ajar and he headed for it.

Vail looked up from the sheaf of papers he'd been sorting before saying, "I hope a night in your own bed's smoothed you down a little bit. When we got off the train here last night you had a temper like an old she-bear that's trying to corral three or four of her new cubs."

"Well, now, Billy, you wouldn't expect a man to feel any too good if he just finished a long train ride late last night and had to show up for work early the next morning," Longarm told him. "Seems like I oughta have a little time just to loaf and maybe sit in on a poker game."

"I'd like that myself," Vail replied. "And maybe we'll both have time for a few hands of poker right after you get back."

"Back from where, Billy? Don't tell me you're going to

send me all to hell and gone on a new case."

"Cases are what you're being paid to handle," Vail reminded him. "And you started this one when you caught Red Collum and brought him in to stand trial for killing Bob Chesterton down in Texas."

"You mean they ain't got around to putting the noose on Collum's neck yet? It was six months or more ago that I nabbed him and brought him in."

"Seven and a half months, if you want to be exact," Vail said. "And four months after, the judge sentenced him to be hanged. But Collum's lawyer's kept busy getting extensions of an execution stay. Of course, Collum had time to learn the ins and outs of the jail where he was locked up, so he figured himself a way to break out. And don't ask me how he did it, because I don't know. But now he's been captured again."

"Whereabouts have they got the son of a bitch?"

"He's out in west Texas, in a little place called San Angelo. And I don't know the fellow who's keeping the law out there. He's the county sheriff, name's Harvey Hudson. Maybe he does a good job, maybe not. But I sure don't intend to take a chance on Collum getting away from him."

"Well, I guess it could be a worse place to get to," Longarm said thoughtfully. "But I reckon you'll expect me to get there yesterday and be back here in Denver tomorrow."

"I wish it was that easy, but just make the best time you can manage. You pick up Collum and bring him back here. And the Department wants him alive, if you can manage it."

"All right, Billy. I'll try, but I won't make no guarantees. Next question is, when do you want me to leave?"

"Soon as you can get ready," Vail said quickly. "I'll have travel orders and expense vouchers for you before today's out. You'll have to take a night train, so you've got plenty of time to make whatever arrangements you need to take care of before you hit the road."

"Now, that's real thoughtful of you, Billy," Longarm said. "And I'll be ready to go soon as I get my travel vouchers."

In the waiting room of the big Denver depot there was the usual late-afternoon crowd, which made the high-domed room look like a stirred-up beehive. Longarm was no stranger to the busy station. He dodged through the milling mass of people with long easy steps, carrying his rifle by the throat of its stock, the strap of his necessary bag looped over his shoulder.

He knew the arrival and departure times of the southbound train as well as the track on which it would be moving, and stepped easily along. Longarm reached his destination just as the locomotive wheezed slowly past him. When the train shivered to a halt he had to take only a few steps to reach the entrance of the Pullman coach designated on his ticket.

Waiting until the last of the arriving passengers had left the coaches, Longarm stepped aboard the car and started down the aisle. The coach was not crowded and most of the passengers were gazing out the windows. Longarm moved easily along until he'd almost reached the center of the car. His eyes were on a vacant seat that was still a few steps ahead when a woman in the aisle seat reached out an arm and stopped his progress.

"You weren't going to pass on by me without even speaking, were you?" she asked.

"Why, Becky!" he exclaimed as he turned to look at her. "Becky Lawrence! You're the last one in the world I'd've expected to see! I heard a little spell back that you'd just about settled down for keeps way up in the middle of North Dakota!"

"That was the idea I had," she replied. "But one winter in that iceberg country was about all I could stand."

"Then where're you heading now?"

"Maybe Arizona or Nevada, later on. But I thought I'd go take a look at Texas first. I hope you're going that far."

"It just happens that I'm going to Texas too," Longarm said. "A little place off to hell and gone named San Angelo. But I don't change trains till we get all the way down to Fort Worth, so we'll be traveling together for a spell."

While they talked Longarm had been covertly studying Becky's face. It had changed little during the time when he'd seen her last: smooth skin that needed no rouge or powder to emphasize its natural healthy hue, blue eyes, a straight thin nose, and full red lips above a firm chin. Her breasts bulged satisfactorily, her waist was thin, her hips full and firm.

"Do I look all that different?" She smiled. "I've been flattering myself every time I look in a mirror that I haven't changed a great deal."

"You're every bit as pretty as you were the first time I saw you," Longarm assured her. "And I'll be proud to be sitting across from you when the dining car opens, that is, if you'll let me take you in to supper."

"You look like you haven't changed either. And of course I'll accept your invitation. We'll certainly have enough to talk about, it's been such a long time since we've seen each other."

When Longarm and Becky got back to the Pullman coach they found that the berths had been made up. Thick curtains hung in front of all the berths, their heavy fabric

21

swaying in time with the sidewise pulsing of the coach. Becky stopped in front of her berth and turned to Longarm with a half-smile.

"I suppose we're facing the age-old question," she said. "Your place or mine?"

"Now, if you don't mind me saying so, that's a fool question," Longarm replied. "We're here, and I'm a ways down the aisle, but if we stop here we'll be getting started quicker."

"As long as there's room for both of us to undress, I don't guess it makes any difference," Becky said, parting the heavy drapes.

She gestured to Longarm to slip through the opening, and followed him into the shadowy area behind the curtains, then pulled them closed and began buttoning the two halves together. Longarm was already sitting down and levering out of his boots. By the time he'd gotten them off Becky had shrugged out of the loose dress she was wearing.

She shed her slip at the same time and when Longarm glimpsed her naked body, ivory-white in the subdued light from behind the curtains, with the budded pink rosettes of her generous breasts, he unbuckled his belt and began fumbling at the buttons of his trousers' fly.

"No, let me," Becky said quickly.

Kneeling between Longarm's knees she brushed his hands aside and started working the buttons free. Becky's hands wasted no motions. As soon as she'd finished undoing his fly she twitched the waistband of his trousers down. Her move freed Longarm's jutting erection and Becky leaned forward to engulf him.

Remembering his past encounters with her, Longarm leaned back on his elbows and watched Becky's head bobbing up and down. She was putting her agile tongue to use now. As the minutes ticked away, the time came when Longarm was compelled to exercise all the control he was capable of in order to prolong the sensations Becky was creating for him.

Minute followed minute while Becky continued her caresses. Longarm enjoyed her attentions as long as he could maintain his control. When he got the first signs that he was nearing the point of no return, he reached down and cradled her bobbing head between his palms.

"I ain't trying to tell you what to do," he said. "But I ain't going to be able to hold back much longer."

Becky raised her head to free him as she replied, "Don't worry, Longarm. I'm sure you remember that I enjoy what I'm doing and I know you'll be longer-winded later on if I keep going."

"Well, I sure ain't the one to ask you to quit," Longarm assured her. "Go ahead and take your pleasure, because I enjoy it just about as much as you do."

Becky engulfed him again and Longarm brought all his control into play while she continued her caresses. After what seemed to be a very long time Longarm was forced to tauten his key muscles. He still enjoyed the acceleration of the rippling sensations that were now driving him into an occasional series of rhythmic quivers, but the time came when even Longarm reached the limit.

As he jetted, Becky's body began quivering and her shivers did not stop until long after Longarm's spasm ended. When at last they lay motionless and spent, she lifted her head and sighed before leaning forward to lower herself onto Longarm's muscular frame.

"I'm really primed up now," she whispered. "Whenever you're ready to start again, just say the word. It's all I can do to wait until I can feel you ramming into me."

"Well, I don't aim to make you wait very long," he assured her. "All I got to do is give you a little bit of body-love, and then we'll go on just as long as we can hold up to it. And the way I'm beginning to feel now, we're going to be tied together all the rest of the night."

Chapter 3

Longarm stepped off the train as it slowed bit by bit and finally eased to a stop at the San Angelo depot. His long trip had been both boring and tiresome after Becky Lawrence had decided to carry out her original plan. She'd gotten off in Fort Worth to look over the growing cattle town and its fast-expanding suburb, the little village of Dallas, with the idea of plying her trade there.

Hefting his necessary bag in one hand and his Winchester in the other, Longarm stood on the depot platform for a few moments gazing at the open prairie stretching away from the railroad tracks. He wondered at first why he was not seeing the town as it had appeared from a distance, then realized that the railroad tracks were on the side of the depot away from the town.

"Old son, you better wipe the sleepers outa your eyes," Longarm muttered. "You still ain't got 'em wide open and it's already morning."

What Longarm saw as he stepped beyond the end of the depot came as a surprise. The case which Vail had assigned to him was only the third he'd worked in San Angelo, and a substantial amount of time had passed since his last visit there. Within that time San Angelo had blossomed. New buildings dotted the main street, buildings that Longarm could not recall having seen before. There were more new saloons than stores, and while most of the buildings were one-story structures still unpainted, he saw three brick buildings glistening-new.

There were a few pedestrians and a buggy or two on the rutted red-dirt streets, but at that early morning hour the town did not show much activity. Beyond the commercial area stretching away from the depot, San Angelo was a town of scattered and generally unpainted shanties. The small ramshackle dwellings filled much of the substantial area between the depot and the terrain further to the southeast. There, the squat close-clustered buildings of Fort Concho dominated the landscape.

At the edge of the fort's huddle of buildings and more readily visible was the stretch of shortgrass fields that served the army post's cavalry units as an area for practicing maneuvers. Even at this early hour there were three squadrons occupying it, taking turns in spreading apart and regrouping into battle formations as they honed their combat skills.

Longarm could hear faintly the barked commands of the officers above the muted thudding of the horses' hooves, though he could not make out the words at such a distance. For a few minutes he stood and watched the cavalrymen maneuvering then, holding his necessary bag and rifle, he went into the depot.

"Do something for you, mister?" asked the clerk sitting at the small table where the railroad telegraph key rested.

"Likely you can," Longarm replied as he pulled the

leath-er wallet in which he carried his U.S. marshal's badge. Flipping the wallet open, he held the badge for the railroader to see. "My name's Long, deputy U.S. marshal outa the Denver office. I'm looking for a fellow by the name of Harvey Hudson. I imagine you'd recognize his name."

"There's only one Harvey Hudson in San Angelo that I know of," the telegrapher answered. "If it's Sheriff Harvey Hudson you're talking about, you better be ready to get set back on your heels when I tell you something."

"Go ahead. I'm listening."

"It was just day before yesterday that poor old Harvey got killed," the railroader said. Then he fell silent.

"Well, damn it, friend, go on and tell me the rest of the story!" Longarm urged. "There's got to be more to it than what you just got through saying!"

"Whatever the rest is, nobody's figured out yet. The way it seems like, Harvey got caught in a standup gunfight. I'd guess it was with some outlaw."

"Well, now, I sure do hate to hear about that." Longarm frowned. "I hope his deputies caught the fellow that gunned him down."

"I haven't heard anything about them catching the killer yet, but Clay Duggan's the man you need to see about that. He's Harvey's chief deputy—or was. And I guess he'll be sheriff till the next election. Anyhow, I heard Clay say before they left that they're pretty sure they know who it was that done it."

"You mean that whoever it was killed Harvey got away scot-free?" Longarm frowned again. "You said they know who it was. Do you mind telling me?"

"Seeing as you're a lawman, I don't see why I'd have to hold nothing back," the telegrapher said. "What I heard is that it was some real bad outlaw Harvey was holding in

27

jail here for somebody to come get and take back to where he was wanted for murder."

"I don't need to know any more," Longarm said when the telegrapher paused. "That outlaw you mentioned, would his name be Red Collum?"

"Now, how'd a man like you from outa town come to know that, and be right about it the first shot outa the box? Why, I didn't hear that killer's name till this morning."

Without answering the railroad man's question, Longarm went on. "I'll just bet a pretty Red Collum shot first."

"So far I haven't heard all about what happened," the railroader said. "But it sure as hell looks like that's what he did. The odd thing about it is that nobody can figure out where that Collum fellow got a gun from. But he ain't likely to kill no more lawmen, not if Clay Duggan gets his way. Duggan and a posse's already rode out. I heard somebody say they're going to catch that Collum bastard or know the reason why."

"How long do you figure they've been gone?"

"Not more'n maybe two hours, give or take a few minutes."

"You got any idea which way they headed?"

"Well, mister, all I can tell you is that I heard some talk amongst the men in the posse. What they said was that this Collum fellow'd likely steer clear of towns or ranches, not that there's all that many of 'em whichever way a man goes."

"What I've got in mind is, in that country to the west of town here, he ain't got much choice except to keep in spitting distance of the river," Longarm explained. "I seem to recall that there ain't any too much water hereabouts, except for the Concho River."

"You talk like you know what it's all about," the railroad

man replied. "Sure, that Collum fellow'd have to keep close to water. I heard the fellows talking about that when they were making up the posse. They figure he's just about got to stay pretty near the middle fork of the Concho."

"Now, that stands to reason," Longarm agreed. "I reckon you've got a map handy that I can look at real quick, without taking time to dig mine out?"

"There's our railroad map in the back room, and the door's right over yonder. It's not locked."

With a nod of thanks, Longarm stepped through the door the railroader had indicated. A quick scan of the big wall map told him what he was interested in knowing. Upstream from San Angelo, where the Concho's middle fork joined its south fork and flowed into the main stream, there were no towns shown on the map. A moment of mental calculating told Longarm that if he angled cross-country in the direction of the stream he had a very good chance of being able to pick up the posse and join it.

Returning to the depot's main room, Longarm asked, "I guess you'd have a place here where a man's baggage'd be safe?"

"Sure. Just leave your gear where it is, I'll see it's put away where nobody'll have a chance to get at it and it'll be waiting for you when you get back. Or am I wrong about you figuring to set out after the posse?"

"You're dead right, that's sure what I'm aiming to do, if you'll tell me where's the nearest place I can hire a horse."

"Stapleton's livery stable's only a hop, skip, and jump past the depot, down through town. He'll fix you up in a jiffy."

"Much obliged," Longarm said. "I'll just dig out what I figure to need from my bag and be on my way."

Hunkering down beside his bag, Longarm opened it and

took out a generous handful of rifle cartridges and another handful of reloads for his Colt. He closed it and with a farewell nod toward the railroad man, stepped out of the depot and took the street leading to the double line of stores that stood along it only a short distance away.

As Longarm had rightly judged, the livery stable stood near the point where the buildings along the rutted street grew smaller and shabbier. There was only one man inside the stable; he was sitting on an upended nail keg, whittling a scrap of wood. He looked up when Longarm entered.

"Howdy, stranger," he said. "You looking for somebody?"

"You'd be the one I'm looking for, if your name's Stapleton and you're in charge here. What I need's a good saddle horse that'll hold up even if I got to push it a little bit. And a canteen that'll hold enough water to tide me over a while if I got to get away from the river."

"Well, that's not a lot to ask," the stableman said as he stood up. "I reckon I can fix you up all right. From what you're asking for and the way you got of talking, I got me a sorta idea you're a lawman of some kind. And I'll stake a dollar against a plug of chawing tobacco that you're going out to join up with that posse looking for whoever it was killed Sheriff Hudson."

"That's a bet you'd win without showing cards," Longarm told the liveryman. "My name's Long, outa the U.S. marshal's office in Denver."

"I'm Stapleton," the liveryman said. "And you know, Marshal Long, I'd be doing the same thing you are right this minute if I didn't have this place here to tend to."

He picked up a saddle and blankets from a sawhorse and started toward the stalls that lined the opposite side of the barn. He stopped after passing two of the stalls where horses

30

stood stamping a hoof now and then. At the third stall he turned to Longarm.

"I'm going to saddle this fellow up for you," he said. "He's a strong one, answers to his name, it's Rocky. He's about the most biddable animal I got left. Them possemen took most of my best riding nags when they was getting fixed up to go out with Clay Duggan."

"As long as your Rocky horse ain't given to foundering or going lame I guess I can make do with him," Longarm said. "And if there's anything special I need to look for along the river—that's where I hear the posse headed when it rode out—I'd appreciate knowing about it."

"Well, you're right about the possemen going along the river, and since they'll be riding across all that dry land out there I reckon you know why."

Longarm nodded. "Sure. I can about hold my own at tracking and following sign. What I'm talking about is places where a fellow like the killer can hide out."

"Why, there's more places to hide than I could tell you about between sunrise and sundown," Stapleton answered. "I guess I could talk about 'em for the rest of today. But none of 'em is exactly hid away, and I figure you're smart enough to find most of 'em."

By this time the liveryman had finished tightening the horse's surcingle. He straightened up and led the horse out of the stall to start fitting its saddle and bridle leathers. Working by the feel experience brings, he turned his head to address Longarm again as he moved to the horse's head to fit its headstall.

"Outside of the fellow you're after, about all you'll need to look out for is Clay Duggan," he went on. "I ain't one to run people down, especially when they ain't around to speak up for theirselves, but once Clay gets a bit in his teeth he's like old Rocky here, a mite likely to stomp and kick a

31

lot, if you take my meaning rightly."

"I reckon I do," Longarm said. "And thanks for the tip. Now, I'm going to sign a government voucher and leave it with you. When I get through with this horse and bring it back to you, we'll fill in the blanks after we've put our heads together about what kind of price you put on renting it and the saddle gear. Then you just take the voucher to the bank and they'll give you however much it says."

"Seeing you and getting a look at your badge is all I need to trust you, Marshal Long," the liveryman replied. He gave the girth strap a final tug as he continued. "This nag's as ready as it'll ever be. You can ride out whenever you feel like it, and I sure hope you get caught up with the posse in time to help 'em grab off the son of a bitch that killed poor old Harvey Hudson."

"Maybe you can help me do that," Longarm suggested. "Did you hear them possemen talking specially about where they were going? Because there's a powerful lot of country out there once you get away from town, and it's been a long time since I was in these parts last."

"What they was talking about mostly was riding to and fro between the river forks," Stapelton answered. "The Concho's got three of 'em, but the easiest traveling's between the north fork and the middle fork."

"That's what it looked like to me when I was studying that big map back at the depot," Longarm said. "Mexico is where I'd bet he's heading. Now, I know I'll have to have water, so I figure to just cut south from here and try to pick up a trail along the Concho's middle fork. If my luck ain't good that way, I'll switch south and see if I might not run into him along the south fork."

Stapleton nodded. "Now, I can't talk for Clay Duggan and his posse, but was I in the lead of it, I'd forget the country in between the middle of both them forks and work along the riverbanks upstream. Was I to do that, I'd sure look to find tracks."

"That's just about what makes sense to me," Longarm said. "So I'll just be on my way, and thank you for all the help you've give me."

Leading the horse out of the stable door, Longarm swung into its saddle and reined it past the fort in a wide sweeping half circle toward the open land beyond. Keeping his mount to a steady pace, he'd soon left the buildings of San Angelo behind him. He zigzagged in wide sweeps as he rode, flicking his eyes across the generally barren terrain.

His earlier cases in the sprawling expanse of Texas had brought him only twice to the vicinity of San Angelo. He'd had no reason before to enter this part of the desert country that covered the region's southwestern sweep. His horse forged slowly ahead, and he soon passed the last straggled patches of ground where grass sprouted and entered the desert area.

Tan was Longarm's first impression of the vista ahead. The light yellowish hue of sandy ground surrounding him was broken only here and there where clumps of stunted cholla cactus formed a dark green blot on the arid yellow soil. Occasionally a lizard scuttled away in an almost invisible streak when the soft thudding of the horse's hooves disturbed the usual quiet of the desert's solitude.

Several times Longarm's sharp eyes detected the hoof-prints of a horse or mule, but the depressions in the constantly shifting sands might have been made by either of them. The night winds had swept sand into the hoofprints and destroyed their contours and depth.

"Old son," Longarm muttered as he reined in, fumbled a cigar and match from his shirt pocket and flicked his thumbnail across the match head to light it, "there's almost more damn country down here in Texas than a single-handed man can handle easy. You better—"

Longarm stopped short, the flaming match in his hand still inches from the tip of his cigar, his eyes riveted on a long shoulder of the dune that rose like a flattened loaf of bread from the otherwise level expanse of sand. Without shifting his gaze he flicked the burning match away and leaned forward to grasp the throat of his Winchester's stock. Pulling the rifle from its saddle scabbard, he rolled out of his saddle, twisting to land on his feet behind his horse.

Longarm dropped to his knees and peered under the horse's belly in the direction of the dune while raising the rifle butt to shoulder it as a man stood up behind the sand dune. He had both arms lifted, a rifle in one of them, the other waving frantically.

Then the man called, "Don't shoot! I'm a lawman, not an outlaw!"

"I guess you got a name?" Longarm called back.

"Damned right, I have!" the man shouted. "It's Duggan, Clay Duggan! And I'm the acting sheriff of Tom Green County! Now suppose you tell me who the hell you are!"

"Long's my name, deputy U.S. marshal!" Longarm answered. "So I reckon that puts us on the same side!"

As he spoke, Longarm was getting to his feet. He stepped around his mount's rump, still holding his rifle ready, and watched the man who'd emerged above the shelter of the rising ridge of sand. Like Longarm, he held his rifle across his body at a slant. For a moment the two men stood motionless, studying one another. Then, moving slowly across the loose shifting sand, they began walking to bring themselves closer together.

Though Longarm allowed no shadow of his feeling to

show in his expression, he was not sure he liked what he was seeing. Duggan's face was bloated and flushed red, his wide flat nose almost purple between high cheeks that bore a tracery of tiny red veins. Although he was not grossly fat, the fingers of his hands looked like small sausages as he grasped the rifle across his protruding belly. When he and Longarm were standing face-to-face, Longarm shifted his rifle to his left hand and extended his right hand. Duggan did the same and gave a perfunctory shake.

"Seems like to me that we was both being a mite previous," Longarm said at last. "But taking your word that you're a lawman just like I am, we got to look out for ourselves, because nobody else is about to."

"If you want to look at my badge . . ." Duggan said.

Longarm shook his head. "I got no reason to doubt your word's good," he answered. "Just like you didn't start off with saying you wanted to look at mine. I figured you'd have one, or you wouldn't try to pass yourself off as being who you say you are."

"You calling me a liar?" Duggan said suddenly.

"Not so's you'd notice. Just sorta trying to clear things up between us."

"I didn't know there was anything to clear up," Duggan said. "Unless you've come all the way here to claim that prisoner that got away from our jail."

"Oh, he's the one I come for, all right," Longarm told him.

"Well, you're going to play hell getting him," Duggan snapped. "That bastard killed our sheriff, and I'm going to see he swings on a gallows!"

"Now, hold on just a minute!" Longarm remonstrated. "If you got any ideas—"

"No, you hold on!" Duggan broke in. "Red Collum's going to stay right here and stand trial, and when the judge says he's guilty and is going to be hung up on the gallows, I aim to be the man that springs the trap!" Duggan's right hand was now resting on the butt of his holstered revolver. "And if you want to settle things, go for your gun and we'll wind up this fuss right now!"

Chapter 4

Longarm was careful not to move a single muscle following Duggan's threat. He stood as though he'd been frozen in place, his face void of any emotion. His eyes moved almost imperceptibly as he watched for the involuntary signals: a tautening of Duggan's gun hand and an almost unnoticeable flicking of his eyes which would warn him that the infuriated chief deputy was on the razor edge of drawing his revolver.

For almost a full minute after Duggan's angry explosion the silence between the two men remained unbroken; then Longarm replied to the chief deputy's outburst. He kept his voice at a conversational level and free from any hint of a threat as he said, "You know, Duggan, drawing down on me ain't going to get either one of us much of anything but killed."

When the tenseness did not leave Duggan's stance and he made no reply, Longarm went on. "Maybe I tromped on your toes a mite too hard, but I sure didn't aim to. Now let's forget about anything but what we're both here for, which is to catch up with that damn slippery Red Collum."

"I reckon I got to admit that what you said makes sense," Duggan agreed before the silence had drawn the nerves of both men almost unbearably taut. The anger and threat had left his voice now.

"I'm real pleased that you'd come right out and say so," Longarm told him. "Because we sure ain't going to get no place squabbling over who's going to take custody of a man we ain't even caught up with yet."

"Well, I put a lot of time into catching up with that Collum bastard when we first taken him in. I got a posse put together to help me find him, but you know how posses fall apart after a day or two. Till you showed up, I was aiming to take all the credit there is for being the one that brings him back."

"Oh, I ain't trying to take away any credit that belongs to you," Longarm assured Duggan. "But we'll both be going back with what the little boy shot at if we don't get to moving real soon. Now, you know better'n I do how the land lays hereabouts. The main thing Collum can't do without is water, and I got a pretty good hunch you'd know whereabouts the nearest place is where he could find some."

"You've got that nailed down right, because the river's about the only place a man can depend on around here," Duggan said. "And right after he'd busted out of jail, Collum was running fast as he could. I'd say he didn't have too much of a chance to stop and fill up a canteen or water bag."

"Maybe somebody on the outside of the jail was helping him," Longarm suggested.

"It'd be a long shot, but maybe you're right," Duggan said. "But let's just say he did have a water bag or a canteen. He won't be toting enough water for him and his horse. Even if he lets the horse go dry, whatever water he might manage to find wouldn't last him too long."

"Well, what's your guess then?" Longarm asked.

"There's just two ways I could see Collum going," Duggan replied. A thoughtful frown was forming on his face as he spoke. "He could cut to the southeast and pick up the San Saba River in a long day's ride. Or he could go the other way and try for the Pecos, but it'd take him a good two days to get to it."

"You figure he'd know how to find either one?"

"Don't forget we had Collum in jail better'n a week, and he wasn't the only prisoner there. He had all that much time for the other prisoners to give him some sort of idea about how the land lays hereabouts."

Longarm nodded agreement. "Well, that brings us up to the next ten miles. You figure cutting for the San Saba River's our best bet?"

"You mean you're aiming to ride with me?"

"I sure ain't going to stay here and plant a crop while I wait for you to do what's my job."

"Hold on now!" Duggan snapped. "Collum's not your prisoner! He's mine! If me and our boys hadn't brought him in, you wouldn't have no prisoner at all!"

"Which don't apply," Longarm put in quickly. "You're bound to know that when a town or county's or even a state's got a federal prisoner on their hands, Uncle Sam's outfit gets first whack at him. Now, let's us just quit arguing and start riding whichever way you figure's our best bet."

"We can split up and try for both southeast and southwest," Duggan suggested. The sharp tone of anger was fading from his voice as he spoke. "That'd copper our bet two ways from Sunday."

Now Longarm shook his head. "That might make sense to you, but it don't to me. I'd say we pick one of them rivers and cut a shuck to it."

There was neither anger nor hesitation in Duggan's voice as he nodded before saying, "Let's try for the San Saba then. It's the nearest, and I'd lay a dollar to a dime that's where he's headed."

"I sorta figured things that way myself," Longarm agreed. "Our horses have been resting while we wasted our time palavering, so we oughta make good time. You lead the way and set the pace. I'll keep right up with you."

"I got to admit that idea you had to ride wide and loop around now and then sure has paid off," Longarm said.

He and Duggan had been traveling due south for a bit more than three hours. They'd spotted prints in several places where for short distances the impressions left by hooves had been overlapped by those of high-heeled boots. They'd agreed that Collum's horse was tiring, and he'd been forced to dismount and lead the horse for a short distance to rest it.

There was no question about the prints being Red Collum's. They were fresh and clear, their edges still sharp, in addition to being the only marks left in the soft windblown sandy soil. Now, Longarm and Duggan had stopped at the edge of a tiny brooklet that bubbled unexpectedly from the thirsty soil and flowed in a thin, almost invisible trickle a handspan beyond the spot where the two men had hunkered down for a close inspection.

Duggan replied, "Well, I guess a man can be lucky and careful at the same time. I didn't know any more than you did what we might find if we stopped here. All I said was it's a good place to let the horses water."

"And it looks like it paid off," Longarm told him. "From what you've said about this dry country and from what little I've learned about it, Red Collum thought so too."

"We can't be sure he's the one that left these prints," Duggan pointed out.

"Those tracks ain't all that old," Longarm said. "Half a day, a day at most. To me that says Red Collum right out loud."

"Oh, I'll agree the chances are that you're right. And we'd be fools if we didn't try to follow the trail whoever made 'em left."

"Sure," Longarm agreed. "And we ain't got time to let Red Collum get more of a lead on us than he's got right now. We better let the horses have another drink, then we'll get going."

A few minutes later, with the horses as refreshed as their riders, Longarm and Duggan were in their saddles, spread widely apart and riding in long zigzag patterns to make sure they'd miss no traces that might have been left by the outlaw. They were rarely within easy speaking distance. When their search took them far apart they were forced to communicate by using arm and hand signals, a closed fist with its thumb held up for a "yes" and a down-pointed thumb to indicate a "no."

More often than not the signals from both men were negatives, and each "no" sign started its sender to widening the loop in which he was riding until he encountered the fleeing outlaw's trail once more. Longarm realized—and took Duggan's realization for granted—that they were following a trail made purposely confusing by the fleeing outlaw.

It was a frustrating search under a merciless sun, one which gave no promise of ending soon. Their horses were tiring rapidly when a rifle shot from the crest of a high-rising dune ahead of them kicked up a spurt of sand a bit short of the hooves of Longarm's mount.

Glancing at the area ahead of him, Longarm saw no gully

or rising dune that would give him cover. As Longarm rolled out of his saddle the gun ahead cracked again, but Longarm was on his feet now, twisting the reins of his horse to force the animal to drop on its side. As the horse toppled he managed to jerk his Winchester from its saddle scabbard; then he dropped flat behind the prone animal.

Another shot sounded from the still-invisible sniper ahead. Twisting his head away from the direction where the shots had come, Longarm saw that Duggan had already dismounted and was forcing his own mount to lie prone. Raising his head above the cover of his horse, Longarm scanned the barren landscape ahead.

A dissipating veil-thin plume of gunsmoke shimmered above a rise in the hillocky sand dunes that rose a hundred yards or more in front of him. On the level stretch below the rise, between his position and the dunes, Longarm saw a saddled horse. The animal was moving slowly on three legs, holding a front leg above the ground. There was no sign of its rider.

Longarm rose to his knees in order to get a better view of the barren stretch below the long narrow dune which he was using for cover. He'd barely had time to glance at the horse when Duggan's rifle spat. The horse lurched and neighed, a screaming burst of pain, and began trying vainly to gallop.

Another shot cracked from Duggan's position and the animal lost its already crippled gait. Its rump sagged and it began trying to pull itself forward with its front legs. The effort was too great for the crippled animal. For a few moments it struggled to move; then it collapsed and lay on the ground, its sides heaving, the swelling flow of blood from Duggan's bullet wound staining the sand red.

Now an angry yowling yell rose from the dunes behind the fallen horse. Before its resonance had died away a man jumped to his feet. He was bringing his rifle butt to his shoulder as he rose, and even before he was standing erect he triggered a shot in the general direction of Duggan's position.

"Damn it, nobody shoots a horse out from under Red Collum and gets off scot-free!" he shouted as he levered a fresh shell into his rifle's breech.

Moving with incredible quickness, he let off a second shot. Now Longarm's rifle echoed the reports of shots loosed by both Duggan and the man who'd appeared so suddenly. The fugitive's body jerked as both Longarm's lead and Duggan's tore into him. Then he crumpled to the sandy soil and lay motionless.

Longarm did not stir until he was reasonably sure that the fallen man was not trying to draw him and Duggan into a trap. Then Duggan's head and shoulders came into sight as the deputy rose from the ridge of the rise that had been his shelter since the gun battle began.

"I'd say we got him, but it sure don't make me any too happy to admit it," he called to Longarm. "Damn it, I wanted to take that son of a bitch alive and see him dangling from a noose on the gallows!"

"Well, now," Longarm said as he lowered the butt of his rifle stock to the ground and levered himself to his feet. He cradled his rifle in the crook of an elbow as he took out a cigar and clamped it between his teeth. "Seeing as how we didn't lose that Red Collum, I'd say that you and me worked things out pretty good after we got acquainted."

"I'm not complaining," Duggan replied. He was on his feet now, starting to lead his horse toward Longarm.

"No more am I," Longarm said. "At least I ain't going to have to watch him like a hawk on my way back to Denver. We done what we set out to do, and I guess that's just about all she wrote."

● ● ●

"Now, wait up just a minute, Billy!" Longarm protested. "It wasn't me that let Red Collum break outa jail! And it wasn't me all by myself that shot him! If you'll go over that report I just handed you, why you'll see it was me and that chief deputy down at San Angelo that caught up with him and it was the deputy that shot to kill!"

"I told you that I wanted Collum brought back alive!" Vail snapped. "Why didn't you stop that local lawman from shooting?"

"Rein in and be reasonable, Billy!" Longarm said. "How was I to know that the deputy'd shoot to kill? There I was with Collum in my gunsight, and before I could get off my shot, the other fellow'd already triggered his, and Collum was toppling over, deader'n a doornail!"

Vail's voice was no longer angry when he said, "Maybe I was a mite too hard on you, Long. But before I'd even had any sort of report from you I had two messages on the overnight telegraph wire from Washington asking why Red Collum was killed instead of being taken alive."

"Well, now, Billy, don't you think that's a sorta tomfool question? Ain't them people that lives back East got any idea about how hard it is to move around out here sometimes? Why, me and that local deputy had to get all the way back to San Angelo from out on the desert, and that took two days' time."

"Oh, I understand that, Long," Vail replied. "But things have a way of looking different when you're sitting behind a nice polished desk in Washington instead of on a horse in Texas riding out to face a killer."

"What do them high-collared starch-shirt nabobs back East figure for us to do?" Longarm asked. "Go up to a killer like Red Collum and ask him all nice and polite to please hand over his gun like a good little boy? Why, they ain't got any more idea than Adam's off-ox about what it's like down there in that desert part of Texas. Come right down to it, maybe they don't know what it's like anyplace but behind a desk."

"Maybe they don't at that," Vail replied. "I sometimes wonder myself. Because just after I got those wires about Red Collum, and how you ought to be criticized for killing him instead of bringing him in to be hanged, I got another message on the overnight wire about you."

"You mean they've heard about me all the way back in Washington? Know my name and everything?"

"Don't get all excited, Long," Vail replied dryly. "The message just told me to put my best man on this case you'll be going to work down in Texas. Seems they're afraid our men there might be so close to things that they can't see the forest for the trees."

"Texas again, Billy? When I just got back from there?"

"Oh, it's Texas again, all right," Vail replied. "But you'll be in a part of it that's a lot different from that hot dry desert country you just got back from."

"Maybe you'd better tell me what part of Texas that might be, Billy."

"It's just about in the middle. I guess you'd know where the state capital is?"

"Why, Billy, you oughta know I ain't a full dumbbell. Sure, I know where the capital is. It's in Austin. And I know it's just about in the middle of things, between San Antonio and Fort Worth. And I've worked cases in both of 'em, if you'll recall."

"Oh, I recall, all right," Vail nodded. "And one of the things that comes to mind right off is that on one of your cases down there you got crossways with a bunch of Texas Rangers, and damned near cost both of us our jobs."

"Well, I still say I was right about that case. But that's not here nor there. What're the big muckety-mucks in Washington getting us into this time?"

"I just wish I knew all the ins and outs of it, but I haven't got the Washington file from back East yet. It ought to be here inside of a day or two, and I've got a pretty good idea you're a little bit frazzled out from all that desert country you've been chasing over. Suppose you just use some of the leave time you've been piling up, and loaf around town until that Washington file gets here?"

"There sure ain't anything I'd rather do than that. I can put in my time catching up on a few little chores I been putting off, like getting my guns looked at."

"I never knew you to have a gun that was in bad shape," Vail said with a smile.

"I didn't say they were in bad shape, Billy," Longarm protested. "Thing is, it's been three or four months since I had Old Man Schroeder make sure they were all right. I figure it's time for him to give 'em a going-over, so I'll take care of that while I've got some extra time to fritter away."

"That's the best way I can think of for you to stay out of trouble," Vail said. "And while you're at Schroeder's, be sure to give him my regards."

"I sure will," Longarm said. "And I can't think of a better way to stay out of trouble than by stopping in at his shop."

Mid-afternoon found Longarm tapping at the door of the gunsmith's shop. After a long wait the door opened and a smile broke over Schroeder's bearded face when he saw Longarm.

"So you at last come to see an old man again," the gunsmith said. "It is a long time since I see you, Longarm."

"Oh, I been out on a lot of cases that took me outa town," Longarm explained. "And I got another one coming up, so I figured I best be sure my guns are in good shape."

"Vich gun gives you trouble now?"

"Well, I ain't got no real trouble," Longarm replied as he responded to Schroeder's gesture to step inside. "At least not none I know about. But like you said, it's been a while since you looked over my guns, and I figured if anything was about to go wrong with one of 'em, I better have you fix it before I get into a jackpot and need 'em."

"Best time to stop trouble is before it starts," the gunsmith stated. "Come. Ve go to vorkshop."

They'd reached the end of the short hallway and started down the short flight of stairs that led to Schroeder's basement workshop. It was a cavernous room, though the cellar looked smaller than it actually was, cluttered with three workbenches and a half-dozen stands holding rifles of all makes and descriptions. A foot-powered lathe and a vat of blueing fluid took up the space along one wall.

Schroeder gestured for Longarm to lay his weapons on a workbench that was the least crowded. Longarm placed his Winchester on the bench, followed it with his Colt, then dug out his ace-in-the-hole, the little derringer that he carried in a shallow soft leather sheath hidden behind his belt buckle. The old gunsmith picked up the derringer first and began examining it, holding the weapon close to his face.

"Ve start small," Schroeder said. He picked up the derringer, took out its two loads and began examining it closely, peering into the weapon's stubby barrel before resting it on his palm and pointing to its smooth-plated sides.

"Chust a spot or two of rust," he said. "So I fix it fast, vit my new cold-plate nickel."

Laying the derringer aside, he picked up the Colt and ejected its cartridges before removing the cylinder. Holding the weapon's butt close to the nearest lamp, Schroeder put his eye to the muzzle and revolved the pistol slowly. Then he shook his head.

"This vun you use most," he said. "I vonder you hit vat you aim at. Rifling grooves bad vorn."

"It still carries true," Longarm told him. "At least, ain't had no trouble with it so far."

"Time to stop trouble is before it starts," Schroeder admonished. "You vill meet no trouble ven I finish. Leave with me the pistol. I have it ready for you tomorrow."

"Hold on," Longarm told the old man. "Even here on my home grounds I'm still on duty, and I'm likely to need that Colt."

"Do not trouble yourself," Schroeder replied. "I lend you a Colt chust like the one you carry. The rifle, I look at later und do vat might be needed."

"Suits me," Longarm nodded. "I'll stop by and pick up the guns sometime before supper."

Leaving the gunsmith's shop, Longarm started back to the Federal Building. He did not see the skulking figure who was following him.

Chapter 5

Longarm glanced at the sun's position as he left Schroeder's workshop and started toward Champa Street. His glance showed him that the glowing orb was at the midpoint between noon and sunset. Turing into Champa Street, he began strolling leisurely toward Colfax and the Federal Building at the apex of that much-used thoroughfare. He neared the end of the wide street and turned into the narrow alley which was a common shortcut taken to their offices by government employees.

Longarm had covered almost half the distance to the imposing Federal Building when an almost inaudible clinking of metal against metal sounded behind him. He could think of only one place from which the faint noise had come, a cluster of a dozen or more garbage pails that he'd passed several paces back. His reaction was triggered as much by instinct as it was by the light clinks which had sent him the message that he was being followed. Longarm wheeled around instantly, his hand going to his borrowed Colt as he turned.

When he saw the menacing barrel-tip muzzle of a sawed-off shotgun slanting upward behind the array of tall garbage pails, Longarm's moves were more instinctive than planned. During his service as a U.S. marshal, he'd been the target of enough backshooters and ambushers to have learned that the best way to handle them was to counterattack without delay.

He dropped to the ground, sliding his Colt from its holster as he let himself fall. He'd barely landed on the ground when the blast from the shotgun echoed between the backs of the buildings that lined the narrow alley. Longarm heard the rattle of buckshot on the tall metal rubbish cans that were shielding him, but lying prone as he was, he could not see his unknown assailant.

Longarm was too combat-wise to waste a shot by firing in response to the shotgun blast. A quick scanning of the clustered waste containers disclosed no motion, no silhouetted figure above the tops of the big metal barrels. The only sign he saw was a thin wispy cloud of gunsmoke shivering in the clear air as it rose above the tall rubbish barrels.

Levering himself to his knees, moving carefully to avoid giving away his position prematurely, Longarm held his fire. Instead of raising his head above the tops of the cans that were providing him with an improvised shelter, he pushed one of the tall pails toward the center of the narrow alley. His careful move of the container opened a small crack through which he could peer.

In the limited range of vision the slit provided, Longarm stared toward the spot where he'd glimpsed the backshooting ambusher's weapon a few moments earlier. This time he saw no movement, nor was the shotgun's barrel still visible.

"He's got to still be there, old son," Longarm muttered as he tried vainly to increase his field of vision without rising above the tops of the garbage cans. "Was he to've turned and run, there ain't no way I could've missed seeing him or hearing him. If he ain't hiding in back of that there clutter of cans, I'd answer right off was somebody to call me a monkey's uncle."

As though to prove that his judgment was correct, a faint scraping and metallic tinkling sounded from the direction in which Longarm had been looking. Longarm shifted quickly from his kneeling position, gathering his feet under his buttocks, ready to spring up the moment he could see a target.

By this time the metallic noise coming from the area where Longarm's unseen and still-unknown enemy was hiding had died away. Experienced as he was in meeting and thwarting the attacks of outlaws and gunmen, Longarm instantly grasped the meaning of the faint sounds. His unseen, unknown adversary was slinking in and out among the garbage containers, trying to get into a spot where he could loose a telling shot.

Longarm saw no reason for changing his own position. He concentrated on listening to the slight noises that his ambusher was making. He was counting on his ears now to locate the position of his invisible attacker, but before his effort was successful the small clinking scrapes had stopped. To Longarm, the message was as clear as though it had been written on a sheet of paper in large letters. He brought up his gun hand, ready for his hidden assailant's next move.

His waiting period was brief. Only an instant passed before the hidden gunman broke cover. It was the moment for which Longarm had been waiting so patiently. At the first flicker of movement from the area he'd been watching, Longarm shifted his position with a half turn. As he moved, he brought up the Colt. When the crown

51

of his attacker's hat rose from the clutter of tall garbage pails, Longarm got the ambusher in the weapon's gunsight and triggered off a shot.

His revolver's sharp crack was echoed an instant later by the deeper booming of the would-be assassin's sawed-off shotgun. It was an unaimed shot, for the ambusher was being knocked backward by the telling impact of the heavy slug from Longarm's Colt. The big pellets of buckshot peppered the high brick wall of the building behind Longarm, but all of the slugs had whistled past him overhead.

Longarm did not shift or turn as the load from the shotgun thunked into the wall, a clicking, spatting sound well above his head. The slugs began falling and he heard them pattering on the ground. The noises registered in Longarm's mind, but his attention was concentrated on the silhouetted barrel of the sawed-off shotgun held by his attacker.

It had already started falling to the ground while the man who'd fired it was crumpling slowly. Longarm could see him now, but could not tell whether the man who still held it was dead or alive and badly wounded. The question in Longarm's mind was quickly resolved when the man, still clinging with a death-grip, suddenly toppled and fell facedown in a lifeless sprawl across his useless weapon.

For a moment Longarm remained in his motionless crouch; then he rose to his feet, his eyes still glued to the outline of the prone and motionless figure lying on the ground. He did not move nor turn his eyes away when the shrill warbling tootle of a police whistle sounded from the street beyond the alley's entrance. Even then Longarm did not holster his revolver, but stood in the same stance that he'd taken when his exchange of shots with the dead man had ended. Now footsteps thunked at the entrance to the alley and a uniformed policeman came running into the narrow passageway. He saw Longarm standing with his still-unholstered Colt in his hand.

"Drop that gun!" the policeman called. "And don't try any tricks, or I'll shoot!"

"Don't worry!" Longarm called. He did not obey the order to drop his revolver. "I'm a lawman like you are, so you and me's on the same side. My name's Long, Custis Long, and I'm a deputy U.S. marshal. I was heading for the Federal Building when that dead fellow laying there tried to kill me."

"Long, you said your name is?" The policeman frowned. "You wouldn't by any chance be the fellow they call Longarm?"

"That's right. If you'll let me get out my wallet, I'll show you my badge."

"No need," the officer replied. "I'm Bill Cox, and even if I'm new on the force here in Denver, I've heard quite a bit about you. Maybe you'd like to tell me about this dead man on the ground here?"

"There ain't all that much to tell," Longarm answered. He began moving toward the policeman as he spoke. "I might know him, but I might not, because I never did get a good look at his face. I was going down this alley. I reckon you'd know it's a sorta shortcut to the Federal Building?"

"Oh, sure. The sergeant that broke me in on this beat showed it to me."

"Well, I heard that dead man there traipsing after me. Then I saw him level out that sawed-off scattergun, and I didn't figure my time had come yet. I drew down and shot him before he triggered off his shotgun."

"Without knowing who he was?"

"I didn't need to know, Bill, not after he pulled that sawed-off out from under his coat," Longarm replied. "Wouldn't you do about the same thing I done?"

"I guess I would have at that," the policeman replied. "But now that I've heard what you told me and know who you are, I sure don't have any ideas about arresting you. All I'll ask you to do is to take a look at that dead man and see if you can recognize him. I'll write down in my report how you explained what happened and how it all came about, and I don't expect you'll be bothered again."

"Well, that's real thoughtful of you," Longarm said. "Let's just go take a quick look at him, because I got a hunch he might be some outlaw that I've run across before. He just about has to be, or else he wouldn't've had no reason to be trying to kill me."

Though the exchange between Longarm and the policeman had been brief, a small crowd of curiosity-seekers had already gathered at the entrance to the alley. Only three or four of them had gotten close to the dead man's body, and the policeman waved them away. They retreated without protesting, but they stopped before reaching the street and turned to resume their staring.

Longarm and the policeman stopped beside the sprawled-out corpse. They moved it so the dead man's face was turned upward, his eyes open and staring at eternity. Longarm needed only a single glance to recognize him.

"Sure, I know who he is, Bill," he told the policeman. "Unless I'm wrong, he's called Kress Palmer. I've worked two cases of bank robbing on him and he got jail time for both of 'em. I'd sorta forgot about him, but I reckon he recalled me and was still mad enough at me to try to cut me down."

"Well, I guess that's all I need to know, Marshal Long," the policeman said. "I'll go on down to the signal box at the corner and get the meat-wagon here. If I need to ask a question or two, I suppose I can find you at the marshals' room in the Federal Building?"

"Unless I'm out working a case, you can," Longarm replied. "Even if I ain't handy, I'd imagine you can get whatever else you need from the report I got to make. Just ask the little pink-cheeked clerk at the first desk inside the office door."

With a gesture of farewell, Longarm turned to resume his progress to the Federal Building. He took the stairs two at a time and stepped into the big outer office, but before he'd taken two steps inside the door, Vail had seen him and was calling his name. Longarm had started toward the big double room behind the entrance area which was used by all the marshals in the Denver cadre; now he veered and went into Billy Vail's private office.

As was generally the case, the chief marshal's desk was piled high with papers: legal tracts in blue-bound folders, copies of arrest warrants, sheaves of yellow lined tablet-paper filled with scribbled messages transmitted from Washington, and a few documents at the bottom of the heap which even Vail himself could no longer identify.

"Well, you took your own good time getting back here," Vail said. "I've been waiting for you ever since the telegraph room clerk brought up the messages that had been sent from Washington on the overnight wire."

Vail's reference was to the telegraph line running from the national capital to all the district offices that had been reached thus far by the nationwide communications system, which was still being installed by the Western Union firm.

"But Billy, you told me I didn't have to worry about showing up here for a day or so until you got some new orders you was looking for from the Justice Department," Longarm protested.

"So I did," Vail admitted. "But it looks like I was a little bit previous, because those orders got here on the overnight wire last night."

"And I guess they want me to be down in Texas as of yesterday?" Longarm asked.

"Something like that. So pull up a chair and sit down. We'll need to go over these orders together so we'll both know just exactly what you're expected to do."

"You got any idea about how long that's going to take, Billy?"

"Not an idea in the world, but it'll take a pretty good while, because I'll have to sort out what'll turn into your orders from the rest of the stuff that flows in here without being any of our concern."

"Then I'll make you a deal you can't turn down," Longarm said. "We'll work till suppertime and knock off, and I'll stand treat to supper at that fancy restaurant in the Brown Palace Hotel. Then we can either come back here and finish, or we can put off finishing till tomorrow."

"Damn it, Long, you know perfectly well that dinner for both of us there's going to cost you at least ten or fifteen dollars. I don't see how you can afford it."

"Oh, I'll manage, even if it means eating beans and potatoes for a while. Have we got us a deal?"

"I'd be a fool to turn you down." Vail smiled. "Let me get to work now, because just thinking about sinking my teeth into one of those big tenderloin steaks they dish up there's already making me hungry."

"Well, soon as you get through shuffling around all them papers on your desk, we can start out," Longarm said. "And while you're shuffling, I'll just get a sheet of paper from that little fellow in the main room out there and write down my report about shooting a sidewinder who come out second best when he tried to backshoot me in an alley."

"I got to admit, this place sure trots out a good piece of meat," Longarm told Vail as he pushed back his plate. It held nothing but the bone of one of the T-bone steaks he and Vail had just finished. "Now all I need is a little tot of Tom Moore's best to top off with."

"Why don't we just go down to the bar there at the end of the room and have our drinks," Vail suggested.

"Good idea," Longarm agreed. "We been sitting here at the table so long that my boot heels have just about started growing roots. Suppose you go on ahead while I settle up with that waiter over yonder. He's been looking our way now and again, acting sorta like he'd be glad for us to finish up."

"I'll see you at the bar then," Vail said.

Longarm nodded. He was gesturing for the waiter who'd served their meal to come to the table. He glanced at Vail's back as the chief marshal wove his way between tables on his way to the bar. The waiter reached Longarm's side.

"Your meal was satisfactory, I hope, Marshal Long?" he asked.

"It was good right down to the last bite," Longarm assured him. "And you tell your boss I said thanks for inviting me and my boss to have supper on the house." He handed the waiter a folded banknote. "And here's enough to make a little thank-you for keeping the victuals moving our way so steady."

Turning, Longarm began picking his way between tables as he headed for the bar. When he got within sight of the full-length mirror on the wall beyond the crowded stretch of polished mahogany, he saw the chief marshal near its center. Vail's face was only partly visible behind the wide-brimmed hat worn by the man to whom he was talking, but the man's figure did not hide the chief marshal's gesticulations.

A small wrinkling frown formed on Longarm's face as he wondered what had upset Vail, and he began taking longer steps as he maneuvered his way between the tables. He reached the clear space between the line where the tables ended, and was within a step or two of the bar when Vail saw him and gestured for Longarm to join him. Longarm began weaving between the tables as he started toward the bar.

Chapter 6

As Longarm advanced, the stranger tilted his head to look at him. Longarm frowned, for the face he saw was both familiar and strange. He was still racking his brain, trying to recall the name that went with the man's vaguely familiar features, when Vail more impatiently motioned for Longarm to join him and his companion.

"You ought to remember Cal, Longarm," Vail said, gesturing toward the man standing beside him. "Even if it's been a while since you saw him last."

"Cal?" Longarm frowned as he extended his hand to grasp the hand of the familiar stranger. "Cal Callahan?"

Longarm understood now why he had not recognized Callahan immediately, for the last time the two had met the skin of his friend's face had been clear and had a healthy tan. The face of the man he was looking at now was distorted by curious strips and bulges of corrugated scar tissue crisscrossing on both his cheeks and his jaws. One side of his jaw protruded beyond the other, his ears had been nocked, and a ridge of scar tissue ran around his brow just below his hat brim. Longarm's puzzled frown deepened as they shook hands.

"I ain't aiming to hurt your feelings none, Cal," he said after the awkward pause. "But you sure don't look like the fellow that used to pardner with me down in Austin when I was new on my job."

"Why, I'm just about the same Cal Callahan I always was," the man said as their hands met and gripped. "But I know I don't look the same. That is, my face don't."

"This time you've said the last word, Cal." Longarm still looked puzzled. "I give you my word, I didn't tumble to who you were till you began talking. What in hell happened to you?"

"I got caught by a bunch of damned land-grabbers and claim-jumpers down Texas way," the mutilated man replied. "They was trying to make me into a turncoat."

"I know you can't be talking about the war, because it was already finished when we began partnering," Longarm said. "You're talking about bandits now?"

"Not rightly bandits. I don't suppose there was any of 'em who'd held up a bank or robbed a train or anything like that. But they were crooked enough other ways, so that later on I got to thinking about 'em the way we used to think about any kinds of outlaws. Except the only thing this bunch was interested in stealing was land."

"Now, land's a pretty hard thing to steal," Longarm observed.

"Sure is, but they've found ways to do it," Callahan said. "What they do is hire somebody to do their law-breaking for 'em. Like they wanted me to use my badge to run off settlers that had started little farms on land claims they'd picked out when they migrated to Texas to resettle after the war got finished."

"And you told the land pirates to go to hell, I reckon?" Longarm said.

"Why, you just know I did!" Callahan replied. "But the trouble was, there was about ten of them and I was by myself. I put up the best fight I could, but they kept tight hold of me and hogtied me. Then they begun palavering at me again. I told 'em the same thing, and that was when they begun slashing at me and cutting chunks outa my face with their knives. Being tied up like I was at the time, there wasn't much way I could fight back."

"It's a wonder they let you stay alive," Longarm said as Callahan paused for breath.

"They damn near didn't," Callahan told him. "I was bleeding like a stuck pig when they went off and left me. The boss of the outfit said if I wasn't dead by morning when they come back, they'd finish the job then."

"So you fooled 'em and got away," Longarm said.

"That's about the way it shaped up," Callahan agreed. "I reckon they figured I was done for, but I managed someways to get off the ropes they had around my arms before it was daybreak. Then I loosed up my legs and got away."

Vail had remained silent while Longarm and Callahan were getting reacquainted. Now he said, "Callahan's a well man now, Long. I knew what happened to him, and I knew where he was because his name still hasn't been taken off the marshals' roster. When the muckety-mucks back in Washington came up with this case you're about to leave on, it struck me that Callahan is a man who might be handy to back you up. So I wired him to come to Denver to talk about it."

"Well, even if I still don't know much of what this case is all about, I'll sure be glad to have you working it with me, Cal," Longarm said.

"You'll know about your new case soon enough," Vail

told Longarm. "It's too late to start talking about it tonight, but tomorrow we'll all three sit down and go over things."

"I know you'll call our hands the way you see 'em, Billy," Longarm said. "Now let's the three of us go find a place to sit down with a bottle on the table between us and do a little chin-wagging to catch up on what's happened since the last time we were together."

"I didn't mention it before because I been trying to figure out a way to put it to you without you getting riled," Callahan told Longarm. "But it seems like to me that we're setting out on a pretty good-sized case."

They were standing on the platform of the Denver depot, waiting for the arriving passengers to finish leaving the train that would take them to the Texas capital.

"I figured you had something eating at you while we were there with Billy in his office," Longarm said. "But I knew you'd spill it when the time was ripe."

"Well, I didn't want to upset him or you either. I know you set a lot of store in Billy, and he's been real good to me, holding me on the work roster as long as he did all the time I was laid up."

"That's the kind of thing you can count on Billy to do," Longarm stated. "Things you wouldn't ask for yourself, he's got a way of handing 'em to you when you need 'em."

"Like this case we're on now, I guess," Callahan said. "I ain't missed a pay packet all the time I been off the job, and I know I got Billy to thank for that."

"Oh, Billy Vail ain't going to let one of his men want for anything he can help 'em get," Longarm said.

"So I've found out," Callahan agreed. "It rankled me more'n a little bit to have to take money I didn't work to earn, but if I hadn't had that money come in, I'd be in a lot worse shape than I am now." He was silent for a moment. "All right, Longarm, I've got that off my chest, and it makes me feel better. But I still want to talk about the case."

"I sorta figured you had a bee in your bonnet while we was on the way from Billy's office to the depot," Longarm said. He broke off when the stream of passengers leaving the train moved down the platform and the shout of "All aboard" came from the blue-coated conductor. Then he went on. "We'd best get on board now, Cal. We'll have plenty of time to talk about our orders on the train, before we get to Austin. I don't imagine things in Texas will be too rough for us."

"After what I've got through with, it's going to take a lot to make anything seem rough," Callahan said. "But still—"

He stopped with a sour smile as the locomotive whistle tooted sharply in two short blasts, and motioned for Longarm to enter the railroad coach first. The lurching of the train's start caught them before they'd had time to reach the opposite end, where the last pair of seats stood vacant.

They placed their rifles and necessary bags on the luggage rack. Neither man spoke until they'd settled down on the coach seats as the train moved slowly through the south half of Denver and entered open country.

"I sorta reckoned we'd find a pair of seats where we could talk easy," Longarm said. "Now you can go ahead and pop out with whatever it is that's been worrying you."

"I don't guess it'd hurt much if somebody was to hear us," Callahan said. "But I wanted to wait till we could talk without a lot of others listening."

"This is as about as private as we're ever likely to be on a train," Longarm said. "Go ahead, Cal. Spit it out."

"Didn't you get the idea that Billy Vail was sorta holding

back a bit when he told us about this case back at his office yesterday?"

"Well, now, he told us all we need to know about them land-grabbers that're taking over farms and land claims," Longarm observed. "And he told us how mean them land-pirates are, not that he needed to after I got a look at your face. But we've both worked mean cases before and never let 'em faze us. I imagine we'll manage to hold onto our end of the rope."

"How're you going to hold onto a rope if you can't grab it?" Callahan countered. "There's been more times than one when I've seen a rope I couldn't even reach, let alone grab hold of."

"It seems to me like Billy Vail's tossed you and me both a rope, and then he let go when we caught it. Now, that's what he's supposed to do. His job is to stay in that office of his and run things. But since it's us that's holding the rope now, it's our job to pull it tight."

Callahan was silent for a moment, then he nodded. "It sounds easy when you say it that way. Maybe it is too, even if I don't think so now. But let's see if we can grab one end and hold onto it all the way to the other end."

Longarm nodded and fell silent for a moment or two. Then he spoke up. "But come to think of it, maybe you're right about Billy. I know Billy pretty good by now, and I could tell he was dodging around a bit when he laid it out to us. And that ain't like him. You know it the same as I do."

"He made it sound a lot easier'n it might be," Cal agreed. "At least, that's the way I look at it. And he didn't say a word more to me than what he told us there in his office. Why?"

"Maybe we might not ever know, but I sorta like to have an idea about what's at the other end of that rope I was talking about us pulling on. Not that Billy'd ever put us in a bad way, send us out blindfolded, or something like that."

"As far as I can make out, you're still talking in riddles," Cal said. "Maybe you better dot your i's and cross your t's."

"Well, both of us saw the orders that Billy wrote down in his case book," Longarm explained. "The way they were put down leaves us free to go anyplace in Texas and do just about whatever we damn well please in settling up all them boundary line fusses. Now, that ain't like Billy Vail generally does."

"I got to agree with you there," Cal said. "I just hadn't thought about it that way. Why, when you come right down to it, we're both sorta like chief marshals on this case. Thing is, where do we start?"

Longarm was silent for a thoughtful moment, then he said, "I guess there's just one answer, Cal. Unless I'm wrong, the Land Office in Austin has got a big ledger that they use to keep track of who buys what land where and how much money changed hands. I guess that's the best place we could go to find a starting place."

"Oh, I know about that ledger and I guess we'd better do that, just to be on the safe side," Cal agreed. "But there's one thing I'm certain-sure Billy knows about that he never did mention, and I got to tell you about it before we go making plans."

"Well, spit it out," Longarm said. "I'm listening."

"My name's in one of them ledgers we'll be looking at. Now, if I start using my badge to help me hold onto what I got, me and you and Billy too are all going to be in trouble."

Longarm was silent for a moment, then he nodded slowly. "It'd be a mite troublesome, all right. If I recall rightly, the rule book says nobody that holds the kinda jobs we do is supposed to use his badge to help him take up government land or any kind of federal property or anything valuable like that."

"That's what I'm talking about," Cal said.

"Well, you know I ain't one to get on the wrong side of the law, not as long as I'm wearing my badge," Longarm stated. "So I guess that's just another bridge we'll have to jump off of when we get to it. But I reckon you set a heap of store by that land you're talking about?"

"Maybe more'n I ought to," Cal confessed. "And I'd sure hate to have it go to somebody else, especially one of them land-grabbers that're trying to set up things so as they can get hold of it."

"Let's not make no judgments, Cal," Longarm suggested. "Not till after we do what Billy said and talk to the chief marshal for the Texas district."

"That'd be Stan Walters. You know him, I guess?"

"I've brushed up against him a time or two. He ain't the easiest man on the marshals' force to get along with. But he'd be the one who'll know where the damned land pirates are busiest right now."

"I thought we knew that already, the way Billy kept talking about the hill country."

"I noticed that myself," Longarm said. "And I got to agree, that seems like the best place. But why don't we wait till we get to Austin and do some looking at them big books in the Land Office. Then maybe we'll stumble over what we don't know we're after yet."

Into the semi-darkness of the day coach a thin shaft of grayish daylight trickled through a crack around the edges of the train's window. In spite of its pale hue the light struck Longarm's eyelids and brought him awake. Sitting up straighter to ease the twinges that had crept into his

66

knees and hips and back after a night of sleeping in an unaccustomed and not too comfortable position, Longarm pushed back his hat and peered through the dimness at his seatmate.

Callahan was still asleep, humped up in what looked to be a very uncomfortable position, but one which Longarm decided must suit his companion, for he showed no sign of rousing. Deciding that he'd risk awakening Callahan, Longarm pulled one of his long thin cigars from his vest pocket. He clamped the cigar between his teeth and fumbled for a match, found one, and lighted it by flicking his thumbnail across its head. He was on the third or fourth puff after the tip of his cigar began glowing when Callahan stirred and opened his eyes.

"You mean it's daylight already?" he asked Longarm, his voice still hoarse with sleep.

"Just about. Sun's not up, but it's light enough to see by. The butcher boy'll likely be coming through the cars pretty soon, and I'd guess we can find something to chew on in his basket."

"Just about anything would satisfy me right now," Callahan said. "And I reckon I'll last till he gets to us."

Longarm was raising the shade of the window as his companion spoke, and Callahan leaned toward it to scan the morning landscape. Longarm had already turned his attention to the countryside through which the train was moving. In the clear morning air the rolling prairie was already fully visible. It presented a vista of gently undulating terrain, green now with large stands of tall waving grasses between small patches of barren ground.

"Mighty pretty country, ain't it?" Callahan asked. "I know this part of it pretty good. Folks hereabouts call it the hill country. Prime cattle-raising land, most of it."

"Looks like good graze," Longarm agreed. "But I ain't seen much in the way of steers."

"There's bound to be some out there," Callahan said. "And there'll be some good cropland too. The trouble is, farmers and stockmen are both after the land hereabouts."

"Damned if you don't make it sound like we're going to heaven instead of just a bunch of nice . . ." Longarm broke off suddenly, staring at the terrain ahead.

"What's happening out there that you find so interesting all of a sudden?" Callahan asked.

"You look and tell me if I'm wrong, Cal," Longarm replied. "Because what I see coming at a slant towards the train tracks ain't either farmers or ranchers. I've seen enough like 'em to know. That's a bunch of outlaws heading this way and they're riding hell for leather to hold up this train!"

Chapter 7

Callahan turned his head to stare in the direction Longarm had indicated. After a moment spent scanning the landscape, and without taking his gaze from the stretch of low green rolling hills visible through the window, he exclaimed, "You've sure called the turn, Longarm! I hadn't got around to telling you what I know about the outlaw gangs yet, but that bunch coming at us is one of 'em for sure."

"Then I'd say this is as good a time as any for me to find out what they're like." Longarm was getting to his feet as he spoke. He lifted down the rifle that he'd placed in the luggage rack. He pumped a shell into the Winchester's chamber. "I'd give a pretty to know who it was saddled us marshals with that new Rule 13. If it wasn't for that, we might be able to surprise them bastards."

"I guess I missed the boat someplace," Callahan said. "I don't recall Rule 13."

"Maybe you didn't read it, but I can tell you what it says, then the best thing you can do is forget it."

"Well, go ahead and tell me. Seems like it's got you pretty well riled up, so maybe I better know about it."

"Once you know about it, you likely won't forget it," Longarm promised. "Now, I ain't going to try to tell you exactly what the words are, but what they all boil down to is, if we get caught in a fracas, us marshals ain't supposed to get off the first shot."

"You got to be joshing me!" Callahan exclaimed.

"If you think I am, just look in the new rule book that came out about two weeks back."

"Maybe I'd best not to. All I've got to say is, it's bound to be some damn-fool pencil pusher in Washington. That's about the only place I can think of where there's a bunch of constipated jackasses that'd set up a rule like that!"

"Sure," Longarm agreed. "Except that we ain't exactly in what I'd call hailing distance of Washington, so we can't ask that damn-fool pencil pusher you was talking about if it's all right for us to let off a round or two. If I didn't have to wait for those outlaws to shoot first, I'd be blazing away right now, even if it is long-range and a mite chancy."

"Well, we can both shoot at the same time and share the blame between us," Callahan suggested.

"Oh, I reckon so, but it ain't hardly worth the trouble. Anyways, it's not going to be long before that little bunch cutting away from the rest will be up even with the locomotive, popping at the engineer."

"Maybe even sooner than you figure, Longarm," Callahan said. "As I recall this stretch of track, it's got a long curve up ahead, but not one that's easy enough for a train to make when it's going full tilt."

"How big of a curve is it?"

"Pretty damn big. It'd be something like three miles or more across the open end."

"Then in the middle it's maybe a mile from the trail them outlaws look like they're following?" Longarm asked.

His eyes were still fixed on the horsemen who'd detached themselves from the little band that had continued moving toward the apex of the curving railroad tracks.

"Something like that," Callahan answered.

"Well, it's the kind of a place most smart outlaws'd be looking for, but it ain't the kind I'd pick out, was I heading a gang of train robbers."

"I don't catch your meaning, Longarm."

"Why, it's easy. You take a bunch of men riding into a curve like we're talking about, and if you got one of your own men at each end of the train and one in the middle, you'll have 'em in a crossfire whichever way they might move."

"I never thought about it that way, but you're right," Callahan agreed.

"So let's us split up," Longarm went on. "I'll go up toward the locomotive and you go back to the tail end. Tell the passengers to lay down flat on the floor and stay put till the shooting stops."

"I guess I'm bright enough to manage that."

"If I thought you wasn't, I'd go myself," Longarm said with a smile. "Now, any of the passengers that's got a gun, you tell 'em they can shoot all they feel like, as long as they're sure what they're aiming at. We don't want one of 'em picking you or me off by mistake if we have to get off the train. Not that I think we'll have to, because once we get in place, we can catch them bastards in a real mean cross fire."

"Sounds just like what she wrote," Callahan said. "Even if I don't have a rifle, this old Colt of mine will toss lead a pretty good ways."

"Let's do it then," Longarm said. "But there's one more thing. You hold your fire till I get a chance to try and figure out who's heading up them fellows. That won't take me but

71

a minute. Then I'll get my sights on him and let off my first shot. After that, we'll just pick out the closest ones for our targets and let 'em have it."

Without wasting any more time in conversation, they moved apart. Longarm started toward the locomotive and Callahan headed for the last passenger coach in the rear. As Longarm progressed through the half-empty coach he flicked his eyes to take stock of the passengers.

He got little encouragement from what he saw. There were only few seats occupied, and most of the passengers were women. Fewer than half of them were alone, most sat beside a man. He saw no gunbelts on any of the men he glanced at. About half of the women had children with them, and two carried blanket-wrapped babies cuddled in their arms. After he'd finished his look around, Longarm reached a quick decision. He stopped in the aisle at the opposite end of the day coach and turned.

"You folks listen to me a minute," Longarm called, raising his voice to override the train noises. When he saw the faces of the travelers turning toward him, most of them bearing puzzled expressions, he went on. "My name's Long, I'm a deputy United States marshal. Now, it's more'n likely there's some trouble coming up. If you ain't been looking outa a window, you wouldn't've noticed, but there's a bunch of outlaws fixing to stop this train we're on and hold it up."

A scatter of voices followed his announcement, and he waved the passengers to silence. "What I said don't mean you're in for a mess of trouble, not as long as you do like I tell you to. There's another U.S. marshal on board with me, and it's likely the trainmen's all got guns. We'll do our best to stand off the outlaws, but you folks'll pretty much have to look out for yourselves."

"How're we supposed to do that?" one of the men called.

"First thing is, don't get spooked," Longarm answered quickly. "What you'd best do is lay down flat in the middle of the aisle here. Any of you men that's carrying guns, hunker down at a window and do what you can to help us stop the bandits. Wait'll they get close and don't waste none of your lead."

"I got a pistol," one of the male passengers called. "But I ain't what you'd call a crack shot."

"Then try for the outlaws' horses," Longarm called back. "They're easy targets and if the outlaws lose their mounts they can't get away from us. Now, I ain't got time to stop and palaver. You men do the best you can."

Leaving behind him the buzz of conversation between the passengers, Longarm moved to the next passenger coach and repeated his message. Then he stepped into the baggage car. That the train's conductor was unaware of danger became obvious to Longarm at once. The trainman was standing at a short slanting shelf that had been fixed to the car's side, writing in his report pad. He looked up at Longarm.

"Something wrong, Marshal Long?" he asked.

"I reckon you'd call it that," Longarm replied. "I don't guess you noticed that there's a bunch of outlaws getting ready to hold up your train."

"Outlaws?" the conductor said. Though he appeared a bit worried, he did not seem to be upset too greatly as he stepped across the car to a shallow wall cabinet. "That's not too big of a surprise, but train robberies have been fewer and further between since we started carrying these rifles."

"I've noticed myself that outlaws sorta favor robbing folks that don't have guns," Longarm said.

"They've left us alone for a while now they know we'll shoot back," the conductor said as he opened the door of the cabinet and took out a pair of rifles. "A long time, a couple of months at least, but now it looks like they're back in business."

"Well, you sound like you've been down the road," Longarm told the conductor.

"A little way anyhow," the railroader said. He was lifting out a rifle in each hand as he went on. "Just let me pass these guns to the engineer and fireman."

"There's not any guns up by the locomotive?"

"Not so's you'd notice. But there will be, as soon as I get up front to the hog."

"I don't imagine your locomotive men are crack shots?"

"That's something I can't tell you," the conductor replied. "But if I do say so myself, I can hold a bead pretty well."

"Then you stay at the locomotive. Keep one of the rifles for yourself, and don't wait to start shooting," Longarm told him. "Just remember the deputy I got with me is back there at the tail end of the train. Callahan will hold up that end of things, and I reckon I'll just stay right here and take care of the middle. I'd bet a whole string of pretties that we can get the best of that outlaw bunch."

A rifle shot cracked from the prairie outside and the thudding of a bullet hitting the side of the coach echoed dully in its interior.

"We best get busy," Longarm said. "I'll get over to that side door and see what I can do."

"Don't risk opening the door," the conductor advised as he turned to go. "Smash out one of those little panes of glass in that side door by where that slug just landed."

"I was aiming to do just that," Longarm said. "Now let's get everything pulled together before those outlaws get too close."

As the railroad man started toward the front end of the train, Longarm raised the butt of his rifle and jabbed at one of the small slits of glass in the baggage car's door.

It smashed when the rifle butt landed, and before the last shards of glass tinkled to the floor he was sliding the rifle's muzzle out of the opening.

While he'd been giving instructions to the conductor, the approaching outlaws had moved closer to the train, and now Longarm could get the full picture of their strategy. One bunch was heading toward the locomotive, the other galloping to the rear of the string of cars. Longarm moved swiftly, for he saw at once that his opportunity was as clear as it would ever be.

Swiveling the rifle's sights toward the front of the train, he drew a bead on the outlaw leading the strung-out line of three riders toward the locomotive. An instant of fanning the rifle's muzzle was all that he needed before squeezing off his shot. The deadly lead whistled through the clear air to its mark.

As Longarm's fatal bullet went home, the leading outlaw's shoulders jerked at the lead slug's impact. The dead man's grip on his reins locked tightly while he began to slide sidewise from his saddle. Feeling its rider's downward slide, his mount began to rear and veer, turning around on its hind feet. The animal's maneuver brought it sidewise into the path of the outlaws who'd been following it.

Its slowly moving bulk was so great that the two riders side by side and right behind the dying outlaw could not rein aside before the panicked animal crashed into the mount of the nearest one. The body of the dead outlaw bounced sidewise from his saddle and landed across the withers of his companion's horse. Its sudden weight on the reins of the second rider set his horse veering into the mount of the third man, who was next to him.

Without hesitation Longarm grasped the opportunity being given him. In the instant when the collision of the outlaws' horses began he was levering a fresh round into his Winchester. In the little three-horse melee it was impossible for him to miss a target, even without precise aiming. Sighting quickly as he swung his rifle muzzle, Longarm got off two shots while the pair of outlaws who were still alive fought their horses and ignored the job they'd set out to do.

Through the frenzy of confused motion Longarm saw the two outlaws he'd aimed at were still alive, though both were bobbing and skittering in their saddles as they rode. Their unpredictable movements gave him no clues as to how seriously they'd been wounded, and he had no opportunity to pick a standing target.

As they advanced, Longarm fanned the muzzle of his rifle to follow them. Before more than a half-dozen seconds had ticked away, he was convinced that he could shift his sights quickly enough to make his lead count. He let off two more rounds, the shots coming so close that they sounded like only one had been fired. Longarm saw one of the remaining outlaws jerk in his saddle, and knew that at least one of his bullets had at least wounded.

Now Longarm could give his full attention to the other man, but before he could swivel his head to aim, the first shots he'd heard from the rear of the train reached his ears. There were two quick reports, one following the other so closely that it might have been an echo. He turned and glanced for a moment along the curving line of cars, but saw no sign of Callahan.

However, even at the distance he could see diminishing threads of gunsmoke wavering in the still air above the observation coach. He also saw three of the outlaws moving at a gallop toward the last coach. By this time the two riders who'd been heading for the engine were turning back and heading for the coach where he was sheltered. The men were riding shoulder to shoulder. They carried their rifles cross-saddle, ready to shoulder them and help their fellow outlaws when they got close enough to make their shots certain.

Longarm had learned in self-defense to read target angles better than most. He had no hesitation about accepting the odds of distance. Ignoring the outlaws who were approaching him from the front of the train, he swiveled quickly and brought up the muzzle of his rifle as he turned.

Longarm's first shot was short. The slug from his Winchester puffed a spurt of dust from the ground inches ahead of the outlaw who was nearest the tail-end coach. Then the distant report of a rifle shot sounded from Callahan's position in the observation coach and the horse of one of the outlaws approaching it broke stride, then stumbled to the ground, throwing its rider a half-dozen paces as it fell, and sending the fallen man's rifle cartwheeling out of his grasp.

At once the fallen man began clawing at his holster. He had drawn his pistol and was raising his arm when another shot from the observation coach threw him backward as it found a mark in his chest. The outlaw dropped, his clutching hand still extended, reaching even in death for the revolver that had landed on the ground two or three paces in front of him.

Longarm wasted no more time in watching the gunplay develop between Callahan and the outlaw. He heard two shots as he turned away, but ignored them and looked toward the front of the train. The two outlaws were still visible there, but now they galloped past the locomotive and turned to gallop across the tracks; then they were lost to sight.

Meanwhile, the train was slowing down. To save time, Longarm took two quick strides to the end of the coach and levered himself over the coupling. Then he stuck his head out cautiously to scan as much ground as he could see along the passenger coaches as they braked to a stop on the curving track. There was no sign of movement, but the air behind him was carrying a burden of shouted half-audible commands.

Wasting no time, Longarm returned to the position he'd just left. He peered carefully in both directions along the arc made by the shining steel rails that curved beyond the train's locomotive and saw that the depleted band of outlaws was straggling away, streaming toward the road.

Shouldering the Winchester he still carried, Longarm speeded them on their way with a final half-aimed shot, even though he knew he was shooting at extreme range. The outlaws' depleted little cavalcade did not stop, but galloped in a series of zigzags until it reached the point where the rails once again curved toward the road. There the lead rider turned and the others trailed after him.

They were still moving at a gallop when the road curved in an arc that matched that of the rails, and within a few moments the riders disappeared from view. Longarm turned back to the train and peered toward Callahan's position in the observation coach. Callahan was just swinging to the ground from the rear platform. He waved to Longarm and started walking beside the train toward him. Longarm dropped the butt of his Winchester to the ground and stood waiting until Callahan reached him.

"I'd say we handed them outlaws a little bit to think about," he told Longarm. "I left two laying on the ground back there, and from the shooting I heard you must've hurt 'em some."

"Just a mite or more," Longarm replied. "And I don't imagine that bunch is going to give anybody trouble for a while."

"I'd almost bet on it," Callahan said. "Did you get a good

enough look at any of 'em to know who they were?"

"I had my mind set more on aiming than I did on just looking," Longarm said. "But from the way they ran, I'd say they're just drifters trying to get a place in the gang."

"I guess we'll have to load the dead ones in the baggage car," Callahan went on. "Likely we'll find somebody in Austin that'll be able to put names on 'em."

From the door of the baggage coach behind them the conductor said, "Stan Walters or one of his men in Austin likely knows their names. But I'll be mighty obliged if you men would help me get these bodies on the baggage car. If we don't move right away, there's a lot of passengers who'll be mad at us for being late and making them miss their connections there."

"Between the three of us, we ought to manage," Longarm told him. "You just stay here where you are and we'll lift 'em up and you can drag 'em back to wherever you pick out."

For the next few minutes, Longarm and Callahan busied themselves with the thankless task of toting the bodies of the dead outlaws to the baggage car's door and lifting them inside so the conductor could drag the dead men into a corner. The job was soon finished, and they returned to their seats in the day coach.

"I'll tell you this, Longarm," Callahan said as the engine's whistle wailed its "go ahead" toots and the train jerked into motion. "If I had my druthers, I'd be your partner in damn near any kind of case you might get put on."

"Well, I'd say you've got your druthers stretching out ahead of you right now," Longarm replied. "I still don't know all there is to find out about this case, but seeing as this part of the country used to be your stomping grounds, I'll be as glad to have you on it with me as you say you'd be with me."

"Well, seeing as we're both satisfied, what can I do to help you next?" Callahan asked.

"Why, sorta get me acquainted with the way the land lays hereabouts," Longarm replied. "Because Texas is one hell of a big state, and I need to know a lot more than I do now."

Callahan's reply came quickly. "You got yourself a deal. Just look around and ask me. I'll do my best to tell you what's where and who's who, and if I leave any gaps Chief Marshal Walters will fill 'em when he tells us more about this case after we get to Austin."

Chapter 8

"You know, Long, it's not very often that I've gone to ask for help from the chief marshal in another district," Chief Marshal Stanley Walters told Longarm. "But I've heard a lot about you from Billy Vail, and from what he's told me I won't be making a mistake."

"Was I to mess up this case after you asked for me special-like, I'd be letting down you and Billy both," Longarm said. "Which I ain't figuring to do."

"I know that Billy sets a lot of store by you, and you'll have Cal Callahan with you on this case. I know what he can do, just like Billy knows how you'd handle a case."

"Billy and me go back quite a ways," Longarm said. "We don't always see eye to eye on a few little things, but when all the chips are in the pot, you'll find us pretty close together."

"So I've gathered. Every year when all of us chief marshals have our annual meeting in Washington, Billy's got a fresh story to tell me about some caper you pulled when you were working a tough case out of his office."

"Looks to me like I better ask Billy why he goes around

telling tales outa school," Longarm said. He kept his face sober. "All I try to do is get a case cleared away fast as I can without leaving loose ends dangling."

"Maybe so." Walters smiled. "And from what I've heard, you don't stop halfways and you tie up those cases with some pretty fancy knots. But that's neither here nor there. I suppose Billy gave you a pretty good idea why I asked for you?"

"All he really said was that you needed some help clearing up a pack of land-pirates," Longarm replied.

"That's the main job," Walters said. "And we've got to be mighty careful to do it the right way. By any chance, have you heard Coy Barrett's name mentioned now and then?"

"Oh, sure," Longarm replied. "He's the first chief marshal that was sent out here from Washington after Texas got to be a state, and then after the war they sent him back. I recall hearing some talk about him having a mighty big load of trouble when he took over that second time, not just from outlaws, but carpetbaggers and squatters and such-like. Are you saying he ain't dead yet?"

"That's a question you'd better not ask him," Walters said. "Because if you do, he'll give you the tongue-lashing of a lifetime."

"You mean that old Coy stayed in Texas when he left the force?"

"That's right. He bought himself a little ranch out of his retirement bonus and he's still working it, with a lot of help from his son-in-law. But Coy's having trouble. First of all, he made a big bunch of enemies when he held down this job I've got now, and there's a pretty good handful of outlaws he brushed the wrong way who're still around and trying to get even with him."

"They'd mostly be the land-pirates?" Longarm asked.

"Not all of them," Walters replied. "Besides the land-grabbers, there's more than one or two bunches of rustlers on the loose. Some of them are crooked carpetbaggers from up north, and some of them started out being drifters, then took to stealing cattle like a duck takes to water."

"Which bunch is giving you the most trouble then?"

"Sometimes I think everybody is," Walters answered. He was smiling, but it was not a happy smile. "What we've got here is just about as bad as another war. This time, it's the stockmen against the rustlers, the farmers against the land-grabbers, or if you want to turn it around, it'd be the farmers against the stockmen and the outlaws against everybody. In my book they're all trouble."

"And that's what you're figuring we'll be riding right into the middle of?"

"Not just riding into," Walters said. His voice was very firm. "You're in the middle of it right now."

"Well, you won't see me grinning a lot about that, but if it's what me and Callahan were sent here to do, I guess we better get started at it," Longarm stated.

"I've said all I wanted to in this private talk we've had," Walters told Longarm. "So if you'll just step to the door and ask Callahan to come in and join us, I'll finish up in short order and you two can be on your way."

Longarm went to the office door and motioned for Callahan to join them. After they were seated, he turned to Callahan and said, "Just before we got tangled up with them outlaws on the train, you were about to tell me how the land lays. Maybe we better talk about it now, while Chief Walters is on hand to set us right so we won't be taking any turns in the wrong direction after we get on the job."

Callahan turned to Walters, his eyebrows lifted in a silent question. Walters nodded and settled back into his chair, where he sat for a moment in thoughtful silence.

"What I've got in mind might not make sense at first," Callahan began. "But if things are pretty much like they used to be here, the best place we can work from is Coy Barrett's ranch."

"Now, wait a minute!" Walters looked upset. "Coy's already retired from the force, and he's already got enough problems without having his farm turned into a damned battlefield."

"Even if Coy calls his place a farm, it's a range war we're talking about, with the land-grabbers tossed in to boot. I don't see any way to keep Coy out of it," Callahan said. "But he's been a lawman most of his life, he'd understand that."

"And how's Coy going to feel if the land-grabbers set him up as a target?" Walters asked. "Which is what they're sure to do, with that big ranch he's got now."

Callahan replied quickly, "Coy's not one to back away from anything. He'd be as much a help to us as we'd be to him."

"Now, just how do you figure that?" Longarm asked.

"Partly on account of he used to be chief marshal here in Texas," Callahan answered. "And partly on account of he's got the kind of a big farm in the hill country where a war between the farmers and the stockmen is most likely to begin."

"Maybe I'd feel a mite better if you'd set me straight on something," Longarm said. "First you call this place of Coy Barrett's a ranch, then you call it a farm. Right this minute, I got a hankering to know exactly which it is."

"Sometimes I think it's one, sometimes the other," Walters told him. "It seems like old Coy can't make up his mind which he wants it to be. Maybe the best thing for you to do is wait and see for yourself."

• • •

"Well, I got to give you credit for telling the truth," Longarm remarked as he twisted in his saddle to face Callahan. He looped a knee around the saddlehorn while he fished a cigar from his pocket and flicked his thumbnail across a match-head to light the long thin cheroot. "I can see now why folks hereabouts call it the hill country."

"Well, we've been together long enough for you to find out I usually do tell the truth, or try to," Callahan said with a smile. "But I don't see why you happened to mention it right now."

Longarm answered without words, waving his free hand to indicate the vista that had become visible after they'd mounted the long wavering ridge to the crest where they'd just stopped. Ahead of them ragged lines of low blunt-crested ridges rose above wide shallow valleys. In most of the valleys glints of the late morning sun were reflected from the surface of small streams that meandered through the wide clefts. A few small houses were visible, dwarfed by the big barns that rose behind them.

After they'd scanned the rolling countryside for a moment, Longarm picked up their earlier conversation. "I got to tell you for a fact, this place you call the hill country's as pretty as any I've ever seen."

"That's a good part of the reason why everybody wants a chunk of it," Callahan told him.

"And I can't say I blame 'em," Longarm agreed. "I can see why a bunch of outlaws would want a place like this. All them valleys would give 'em a place to hole up in, or even keep rustled steers from straying till the rustlers could change the brands and sell 'em. And there's more'n enough room to hide even a pretty good-sized herd."

"That's the way it used to be," Callahan said. "But the

rustlers never did get around to filing claims for the land they used."

"And the folks that live here now did file claims, all right and proper?"

"Sure. Most of them settled from what all of them call the old country, but whichever country they're talking about had laws these people have been obeying all their lives."

"All of 'em come from different places then?" Longarm asked.

"Well, a lot of the places they're from are pretty well scattered out, but most of the ones that've settled right around here came from Germany."

"How you figure that happened?"

"Why, they're leaving to get away from wars that've been going on a long time, some of them a hundred years or more. And there's a few from Italy and France and some other little countries I can't rightly put a name to."

"Would you say they get along pretty well together?" Longarm asked. "As I recall, a lot of them little countries are fighting each other a lot of the time."

"Most of the settlers hang together without fussing. A lot of them have been in more wars than you or me's ever likely to see. They don't blow up easy, and a few of them have already started to wear gunbelts."

"And do they all join up to fight back when they get a chance at the rustlers?"

"Some of 'em have been in so many wars in the countries they came from that they've had a bellyful of fighting. But there's a few that don't hold back," Callahan replied. "Trouble is, there's not enough of them. They wouldn't be likely to make much difference if they did join up."

"Then don't you think . . ." Longarm cut his question short as he reined in and motioned for Callahan to do the same. He did not speak to his companion for a moment; then he pointed to a small grove of huisache trees that rose behind a thick tangle of dried and drying chamisal a quarter of a mile ahead of them. He did not take his eyes off the trees and the seemingly impenetrable stand of thickly tangled underbrush as he raised his arm to gesture toward them.

"What's the matter?" Callahan asked. He was moving his head slowly from side to side, trying to locate the object at which Longarm was pointing. "I don't see anything but a little stand of trees back of all that brush ahead of us."

"That's all I noticed at first," Longarm replied, still keeping his eyes on the grove. "Then I saw a little flash that looked like a sorta sunshine reflection, maybe off of some harness gear or something of that kind."

"You think somebody's holed up there?"

"There might be or there might not. We been flapping our jaws too free for us to pay much mind to what could be ahead of us. But I'd say we got to start out again right quick. We'd best spread apart as far as we can and still talk back and forth."

Callahan nodded, a quick jerk of his head. He poked a boot toe into his horse's flank, and reined the animal away from Longarm's mount. Longarm toed his own horse into motion once more, his eyes still fixed on the trees. As he rode he slid his Winchester from its saddle holster and balanced it across his thighs between his crotch and his saddle horn.

Longarm's move might have been a spur to the shot that came from the vegetation almost at once. The singing slug that whistled past his head was uncomfortably close. Longarm leaned forward in his saddle, crouching low on his mount's back. Another shot from the grove broke the stillness and kicked up a spurt of dust just beyond the hind feet of Callahan's horse.

Callahan reined aside and began zigzagging as he toed his horse to a quicker gait. Longarm followed his companion's example. Now both men were galloping toward the heavy brush and the trees beyond. Their sudden burst of speed brought another shot from the hidden sniper, but now he had only moving targets. The concealed antagonist's lead did nothing but raise another puff of dust between the two galloping horses.

Longarm was far from being close enough for his Colt to be really effective, but he knew he had more shells for his revolver than for his rifle. To save wasting the loads in his pistol he slipped the Winchester's butt between his thigh and saddle, then slid the revolver from its holster and loosed a random shot into the thicket ahead. The bushes shivered and waved for a moment, then were still again.

"Maybe I got him with that chancy shot, but I don't figure it's too likely," Longarm called to Callahan.

His companion was thirty or forty yards away, and instead of speaking, raised his arm and lifted his rifle up and down two or three times to acknowledge Longarm's call. The gesture drew another shot from the undergrowth ahead. Callahan's horse broke its gait as it whinnied in pain, then it resumed its steady advance.

Longarm holstered his Colt and freed his Winchester. He had no real target, and the rifle's shells were too scarce to be wasted. The distance between him and Callahan and the concealed sniper was too great for him to rely on his pistol, the sniper too well-hidden for him to squander rifle slugs on an invisible target.

Raising his voice, Longarm shouted, "Get in back of him!"

Callahan waved to acknowledge Longarm's call and reined away from the straight-line course he'd been following, to ride on a long slant away from the thick wall of underbrush and small trees ahead. Longarm toed his horse into a slant in the opposite direction.

As they galloped toward the arroyo's edge the trees and brush both grew thicker. Now the more luxuriant growth of chamisal combined with the trees to become a shield rather than a hindrance. Both Longarm and Callahan knew that the vegetation would not stop a bullet, but they also knew that a slug passing through it could readily be deflected.

Their still-unseen antagonist did not vary his pattern. He loosed an occasional shot, but the unpredictable zigzag moves of Longarm and Callahan coupled with the high heavy growth they'd managed to put between them and the concealed sniper combined to baffle their hidden enemy. The gunman still shot, apparently when he could get a reasonably good angle of fire. However, his shots now came at greater intervals, and the accuracy of his aim was still defeated by the dense vegetation.

Now the thick growth through which Longarm and Callahan had been slowly progressing showed signs of thinning and Longarm raised his voice. "Bear to your right," he called. "I'll take the other side. We'll leave the horses here and see if we can get that son of a bitch in our sights for a change instead of shooting blind!"

"You let off the first shot," Callahan called back. "I'll hold my fire a minute before I cut loose!"

"I ain't going to be in no hurry," Longarm informed his companion. "The way I figure is we'll just stay in this cover till we can see somebody to aim at."

Swinging out of their saddles, each man judging his distance from the other by the noises they made as they pushed through the brush, Longarm and Callahan started their advance. They'd covered only a few yards and could still see nothing ahead but more brush when a rifle barked ahead of them.

Only three shots sounded and the slugs whistled and crashed through the bushes high above their heads. Neither Longarm nor Callahan responded. They continued their steady but noisy progress until only a narrow strip of cover remained ahead of them. Through the rapidly thinning brush the drop-off line into the wide arroyo beyond was plainly visible.

Keeping his voice as low as possible, Longarm called to his companion. "You still got enough shells to waste a few?"

"A few's all I've got," Callahan answered.

"Then you take two and I'll take two when we break cover," Longarm said. "And maybe by then we'll be able to see who we're shooting at!"

"That's good enough for me," Callaghan told him. "Say the word!"

"Now's the—" Longarm broke off as the thudding of hoofbeats sounded beyond the thin line of growth.

He stood up and started ahead, shouldering his rifle as he moved. Callahan was also getting to his feet. The hoofbeats began fading as they raced to the rim of the drop-off. In a wide swathe of level land below they saw a rider galloping away.

Longarm got off the first shot, and saw the slug kick up dust from the ground behind the galloping horse. Callahan's aim was no better, his hurried shot also went wild. The fleeing rider was already wheeling his mount behind the shelter of a huge stand of high-growing cholla cactus, and its maze of twisted limbs was as effective as a blindfold in hiding him.

"Damned if we didn't miss the best chance we're likely to get!" Callahan said as he lowered his rifle. Disgust at

90

their failure was reflected in his voice.

"There ain't no way to change things now," Longarm replied. "We had this chance at him, but that ain't all she wrote. He likely won't slow down for a spell, and he'll leave plenty of hoofprints long as he pushes hard. Let's me and you not waste any more time than he did."

Chapter 9

"You're aiming to follow him then?" Callahan asked.

"We damn well better, and catch up with him to boot," Longarm said over his shoulder as he headed for his horse. "It's an outside chance we'll just be letting him lead us on a wild-goose chase, but I don't figure it is one. I'm guessing he's got some other fellows waiting someplace up ahead."

"If that's the way of it, we haven't got much choice but to follow him," Callahan agreed. "But if he's got a gang waiting for him—"

Longarm interrupted his companion. "It don't matter much whether he has or not. Right this minute he's the only bet we got on the table."

Callahan was just a step behind Longarm now, taking long strides to keep up. He hurried to get abreast before saying, "If we run him to ground, we better figure he's meeting up with some cronies. If we run into a bunch of 'em, what're we going to use for shells? I've got some left in my saddlebags, but if we get close enough to some kind of outlaw bunch we'll sure as hell wind up in a shooting match."

"Let's skin that cat after we catch it," Longarm replied. "Right this minute, we better set ourselves to cottoning onto that fellow's tracks. After we pick 'em up we'll have plenty of time to figure out what's best for us to do."

They'd reached the horses now, and wasted no time in swinging into their saddles. Longarm gestured for Callahan to go first, and waited until he'd ridden perhaps a quarter of a mile before toeing his own mount into motion. They rode abreast then, with a gap of less than a half mile between them as they set out to follow the trail of the fleeing outlaw.

It was a slow chase. Each time the hoofprints vanished on a stretch of hard-baked ground both men were forced to ride in semicircles that widened into full circles as they tried to pick up the prints left by their fleeing quarry. In some areas the soil's crust was too hard to break; in others wide expanses of loose shifting sand took prints badly and crisscrossed with other hoofprints made earlier, which confused the trail to an even greater degree.

There were also spots where the blowing of a rare hard night wind had cleared the sand from a shallowly covered rock formation. At each of these breaks their progress was slowed for a time while they rode widening semicircles around the perimeter of the treacherous area in order to pick up the fleeing man's trail beyond it. Their maneuvers often forced them apart, but they persisted, and as the sun dropped toward the edge of the horizon, trailing became a bit easier.

Now its slanting rays created small dark shadows where the shifting sand had been pressed down by the hooves of their quarry's horse. Darkness was just beginning to appear on the eastern horizon when Longarm saw the almost invisible shimmer created by a virtually smokeless fire crinkling the clear air ahead.

At the point he'd now reached, Longarm was still separated by a half mile or more from his companion. Standing up in his stirrups, he began waving his hat above his head. Callahan saw the signal and waved in reply, then wheeled his horse around and started to join him.

By the time the two were together again, only a sliver of the sun's golden arc remained on the western horizon-line and night's deep blue was already taking over the eastern sky.

"If I read your signal rightly, you've had better luck than I did," Callahan said. "I sure hope so, but I ain't too proud to admit that I wasn't much good at trying to find any prints on that hard-crusted stretch I was trying to track over."

"Likely you didn't see any tracks because there weren't any in that direction," Longarm said. He had dismounted and was stretching his legs by striding back and forth beside the animal. "Anyway, trying to pick up prints off of a rock-shelf big and hard-dried as the one you were going over ain't the easiest job a man can take on."

"You can double that in spades," Callahan agreed. "But am I right? You been luckier than I was?"

"Call it luck or anything else that might come to mind," Longarm told him. He gestured in the direction where he'd seen the heat-shimmer of the fire. "But if you'll look quick along thataway before it gets too dark to see anything, you'll spot the same little bit of sign I did."

Callahan turned to run his eyes along the sky in the direction Longarm had indicated, but the deep fast-moving blue of night had already shadowed the eastern heavens. He finished his quick scanning with a dissatisfied headshake as he returned his attention to Longarm. "I suppose I got here too late to see the same thing you did. But if what you saw is good enough for you, it's sure good enough for me."

"All I seen was a little shivery heat-shine raising up. It wasn't such a much, but I'm sure as God made little green apples it was coming from somebody's cooking fire,"

Longarm assured him. "Somebody that didn't want to make no smoke."

"If that sniper's got a supper fire going, I don't imagine he's put it out yet," Callahan said. "Even if he's just let it burn down to coals, it'll be easy enough to spot when we get closer to it."

"It looked good enough to me to figure out that maybe we'll find some rustlers there. My guess is that they ain't leaving right now, because trying to handle a bunch of half-wild steers at night is a job that nobody in his right mind has got a real hankering for."

"We can always stop short of the fire and see what we're running into," Callahan suggested.

"That's how I figure too," Longarm agreed. "And the sooner we start, the quicker we'll get there. I got enough landmarks tucked away in my head to get us moving in the right direction."

"I've got a few I'm keeping in mind myself, so between us we ought to be able to split up and cover a pretty fair amount of ground. Maybe even enough to run down whatever kind of nest the rustlers have fixed up to work out of."

"This ain't time for us to split up very far," Longarm said. "Maybe a quarter mile or so. Now and again you look over towards where I'll be, and I'll keep you in sight, so we can join up quick in case we need to."

"But there'll be part of the time when I won't be able to see you, or you me," Callahan objected. "Especially when it gets full dark."

"Oh, I got that all worked out in my head. I'll puff hard as I can on a cigar and get a smoke-trail going up."

"I hadn't thought about anything of that kind, but I guess I can see your cigar glowing in the dark about as clear as I could a blazing fire. The trouble is, that bunch of outlaws can likely see it too."

"That's the chance we'll have to take," Longarm said. "A cigar tip won't likely be noticed if you ain't expecting to see one. It ain't exactly like a smokestack, even in this clear air. Late as it's getting, I don't figure that bunch is going to start anyplace till tomorrow morning."

"You figure to jump them then, maybe before they wake up?"

"Let's not do no jumping till we're ready for 'em," Longarm said. "And I'd say daybreak's the best time to aim for." He was already stepping toward his horse as he added, "And now maybe we better quit fanning the air with maybes and get to moving."

Mounting quickly, watching Callahan mount and ride away, Longarm stayed where he was until his companion was well along. Then he reined his horse in almost the same direction, but at a wide-slanting angle to the course Callahan had chosen. With a few careful toe-pokes he set his mount's gait to be a bit faster than the one chosen by Callahan, and reined away from his companion's straightforward pattern.

When Callahan looked to be the size of a midget mounted on a child's pony, Longarm slowly altered his direction to ride on a line that would be parallel to the course of his companion.

Longarm had not even tried to keep track of the hours that had passed since they'd set out, but the sky told its own story of elapsed time. On the western horizon the sky still glowed with a narrowing line of the sunset's crimson hue. Overhead the deeper blue of night was pushing slowly but steadily across the arch of the heavens, though there was still enough light for Longarm and Callahan to see one another dimly as they rode across the treeless and featureless ground.

Both men knew that their time was growing steadily shorter. They were riding a quarter of a mile apart or more now, on a long uphill slant. Longarm gave his mount's rump a backhand slap and the tired horse responded with a small increase in its gait. Ahead he could see the crest of the seemingly interminable rise. The upslope was one that a fresh mount would take in stride, but the angle was enough to slow his now-plodding mount.

At last the crest of the rise was only a short distance away and Longarm looked across the stretch that separated him and Callahan. He saw that his companion's horse was making no better progress than his own, and gestured for Callahan to angle toward him. At the same time he slanted his own course to meet Callahan. The two men reined in when they met.

"I got to figuring," Longarm said. "We're close enough to the lip of this long up-stretch for us to finish that little strip ahead on shank's mare."

"And leave the horses here?" Callahan asked.

"Not without one of us stays back to bring 'em up should we need 'em," Longarm replied. "So why don't you keep 'em here long enough to give 'em a breather. I'll mosey on ahead to see how the land lays past the rimrock."

"It's up to you," Callahan said. "When you're ready for me to come up with you, just give a wave."

"Sure," Longarm nodded.

He was pulling his Winchester from its saddle scabbard as he spoke, and with a quick nod to Callahan he started up the short, steep, slanting strip that remained between him and the crest of the slope. When he was within a half-dozen feet of the rimrock's jagged edge, Longarm dropped to all fours and began to crawl. The rifle had become a hindrance, throwing him off balance each time he lifted it. His progress now was slower, but a bit steadier.

At last Longarm reached a point where his head was within inches of the crest. He pushed his hat back, letting it dangle behind his shoulders on its chin-loop. Then he dropped flat and started pushing himself ahead with his boot toes, moving slowly and carefully to avoid making any noise. When he reached the rimrock's edge he planted his hands flat on the rocky soil and shouldered himself upward until he could peer down at the ground below the drop-off.

A short distance away from the base of the cliff from which Longarm was looking, four men were hunkered down around the faintly flickering and dying coals of a small fire. They were talking, and occasionally one of them would raise a hand to make a small gesture, but the light, intermittent breeze that had begun at darkness's onset carried away their words. All that Longarm could hear was an indistinct muttering. Beyond the group he could make out the dark shapes of their horses, but it was impossible to see whether the animals were still saddled.

Before Longarm had decided on the next move for him and Callahan to take, the men grouped around the dying fire began rising to their feet. One of them started toward the horses, stopped halfway to the point where the animals were tethered, turned back, and raised his voice to call to his companions.

"Fonzo, you just remember to spell me when I've done my time being night watch for the herd down there," he said. "If you don't show up, I'll be coming back here to rouse you."

"Don't worry, Carson," one of the men beside the glowing coals replied. "I still say them horses is too tired to stir none, but even if I don't think we need no night watch either here or down by the herd, I'll do my stand down there, just like you fellows said you would."

"You two quit hollering!" another of the men by the fire said. "If we're going to get them steers moving at daybreak, we need what rest we can get right now!"

The man on watch departed. The pair close to the small bed of dying coals got busy spreading blankets, and the third moved a few paces away, where he settled onto the ground in a legs-crossed posture, his rifle across his knees. After a bit of stretching and grunting the pair with the blankets finally made themselves comfortable. A few moments later, snores and deep, low-pitched whistling exhalations gave Longarm the message for which he'd been waiting.

Longarm returned to where Callahan was waiting, and explained the situation. Callahan nodded. "You figure like I do? Let the ones in their bedrolls get sound asleep and jump the one standing watch?"

"Sure," Longarm replied. "That one awake's the one to look out for, and I'll handle him if you want to take on the two that's asleep, or we can go the other way around. After this bunch is corralled, there won't be but the one down below riding night-herd."

"You feel like taking on the two in their bedrolls?"

"Why not?" Longarm answered. "Laying asleep like they are, I got a hand for each one of 'em. Say I give you a couple of minutes to move over by the one sitting up. Then I'll get the two corralled and you put your man to sleep with a pistol butt before he gets time to yell."

"That's what I been thinking," Callahan said. "Then we'll work together on the one with the herd."

No further preliminaries were necessary. Both men climbed up to the rimrock's jagged edge. Then they separated. Longarm moved to the spot where the two sleeping men were now beginning to snore, one loudly, the other softly. Kneeling between their bedrolls, Longarm stretched his arms out to give him a gauge of distance. Then he leaned forward, both arms extended from his shoulders, and when he was sure that he'd judged his distances correctly, he dropped his shoulders and clasped

100

each man with the heels of his palms covering their mouths.

Putting the full strength of his muscular hands to work, he clamped the outlaws' jaws firmly closed while leaning forward on his arms to hold their beads pinned to their blankets. For a moment the two the two rudely awakened outlaws were too stunned to move, then they began tugging at Longarm's wrists. He tightened his grip until he could feel the small movements of their jaws.

"You two lay still," Longarm commanded, his voice harsh. "I don't want to have to bust your jawbones, but that's what I'll do if you don't settle down."

As the threat in Longarm's words sank in, the gurgling muffled gagging noises that had been coming from the outlaws' throats suddenly subsided, then stopped completely as they tried to release themselves by twisting and turning. Their hands went to Longarm's wrists and forearms as they tried to free themselves, but without leverage they could do nothing.

For a moment or two more the renegades struggled to free themselves. Then their inability to breathe freely started sapping their resistance as the oxygen in their lungs was exhausted. They let their arms drop. The gargled noises coming from their throats kept sounding, but they weakened steadily and the outlaws finally stopped the resistance they'd shown at first.

A shot sounded from the edge of the drop-off. Longarm was tempted for a moment to release his holds and draw his Colt, but before he could decide to do so Callahan shouted, "I had to finish off the one here. But if you can hold them others a minute or two longer, I'll be up there to give you a hand, Longarm!"

"I've held 'em so far!" Longarm called back. "I reckon I can hang on a little spell."

As the exchange between Longarm and Callahan ended, so did the struggles of the two outlaws on their backs on the ground. They lay quietly now, their chests heaving for want of air as the last vestiges of oxygen in their lungs were exhausted. Then boot soles grated from the lip of the drop-off and Callahan appeared advancing through the darkness, carrying a loop of rope.

He said, "I'll have those two hogtied in a minute, if you can hang on, Longarm."

"Why, I ain't having no trouble," Longarm said mildly. "But I reckon these fellows need air pretty quick, or they ain't going to be able to tell us what we need to know."

Callahan made short work of trussing the outlaws' arms and ankles. The two prisoners lay supine when Longarm released them, too exhausted to move any more muscles than those necessary to draw fresh air into their lungs. Only then did Longarm release his iron grip. He rose to his feet and stood looking down through the darkness at the hogtied men.

"You can start talking any time," he said. "And I reckon you know what'll happen if you don't tell us who's hired you and where we'll find 'em."

Chapter 10

For a moment neither of the men spoke; then one of them asked, "What about that shot just now?"

"You got to mean the shot I let off," Callahan replied. "Some fellow up on the rimrock was fool enough to try and draw down on me. Even if the light wasn't none too good, I had him in my sights dead to rights."

Now the two captives exchanged glances. The frowns that spread quickly over their faces were Longarm's invitation to say, "All right, you two. After what happened to your partner, you don't need for me to tell you we mean business. Go ahead and start talking and we'll do the listening."

"Talking about what?" the younger of the pair asked.

"For openers, you can tell us the name of whoever's bossing this rustling you been doing."

"Now, don't go making no mistakes about us," the second man said quickly. "I reckon we're smart enough to know when we're beat. But that don't mean we'd be fools enough to blab about who's running things. One thing we found out is that it don't do to talk about the outfit we're hooked up with."

"Then you don't care whether you save your skins or not," Callahan suggested. He turned to Longarm. "Ain't I right, Longarm?"

"It'd sure be nicer if they'd tell us, so we could get started in the right direction," Longarm replied. "But it's full-moon time, so we won't need to worry. Soon as the moon rises it'll be near to daytime-bright, and it won't take long after we've gone on for the wolves and coyotes to smell out these two and come moseying around looking for supper."

"We might as well start out now then," Callahan said. "I'd say we've given 'em all the chance they deserved."

"I got to agree with you," Longarm said. "Let's go back to where we left our nags and get started." He took a step toward his horse, and Callahan moved to follow him. Before either of them could lift a leg to step into a stirrup one of the outlaws spoke.

"Hold up a minute!" he called. "We ain't flap-jaws or squealers and we're used to being roughed up once in a while, but when it comes down to blabbing or making a supper for coyotes and prairie wolves, that's something else again!"

"If you mean what you're saying, we just might think about taking you along with us instead of leaving you to the wolves," Longarm said. "But don't expect us to let you go free, even if you do tell us what we need to know."

"You do the asking then," Callahan said to Longarm. "I'd say the first thing we need to know is these fellows' names."

For a moment the man hesitated, then he said, "I'm Parkins." He stopped long enough to look at his companion, who turned down the corners of his mouth and shrugged.

Parkins went on. "This fellow I'm riding with is Fonzo. That oughta be enough to satisfy you."

"There's some folks says I'm a hard man to satisfy," Longarm said. "Maybe I am, maybe I ain't. But I'll try to make it easy on you if you make it easy on us."

"Meaning what?" Parkins asked.

"Meaning that the first thing I want to know is the name of the man that's boss of your rustling outfit. I'd imagine he's waiting for you at wherever it is you figure to drive that bunch of steers you got to deliver."

This time, Parkins did not reply so quickly. At last he said, "Even if we was to tell you his name, for all we know it might not even be his right one. All we'd know about is the name he generally answers to."

"Why, that's all Longarm's asking you," Callahan put in. "And I got to tell you, he can be a right mean man when he don't get his questions answered."

Longarm said quickly, "Now don't you go bragging on me, Callahan. Let these fellows find out for themselves. But I'll say this much, if they don't start talking there ain't no use to us keeping 'em alive."

"Now, hold on!" Parkins protested. "You ain't gonna shoot us, are you?"

"You ain't worth wasting powder and lead on," Longarm told him. "Not when we can just leave you here for the wolves and coyotes to finish off. You'd likely die slower and hurt a lot more'n you would if I was to plug you, but that's up to you."

"All I know is we was told to drive 'em up northeast," Parkins replied. "Somebody's supposed to be waiting for us and they'll guide us the rest of the way."

"Somebody meaning who?" Longarm asked.

"Why, I don't recall that there was any names mentioned."

"And I'll bet a double eagle to a plugged nickel they didn't say exactly where you was to drive the herd."

"All they told us was to head northeast," Parkins answered.

Longarm shook his head. "That just ain't good enough. Nobody in his right mind's going set you out to steal a cattle herd without telling you where to take it."

There was defiance in their captive's reply as he said, "I know when to talk and when to keep my mouth shut. I've said all I aim to say, and that's that." Turning to his companion, he scowled. "And you better not flap-jaw like you generally do, Fonzo."

For almost a full minute Longarm looked from Parkins to Fonzo. Then he said, "Well, now. I guess I better tell you two men, I got a mean streak in me. When a liar tries to take me in, I just cut out his tongue so he can't lie to nobody else."

"Hold on a minute!" Parkins protested.

"And when a man gets his tongue cut out, he generally bleeds to death," Longarm added. "That's what I meant when I said he won't never lie to nobody else."

Callahan picked up the cue at once. He took his eyes off the prisoners for a moment to glance at Longarm, who returned the questioning look with a nod.

"All you got to do," Callahan said to Longarm as he turned back to the outlaws, "is tell me which one you want to take the tongue out of first. I'll hold him so he can't move around. After the one that's left sees what happens to his friend, I'd imagine he'll feel a lot more like telling us what we want to know."

For a moment Longarm did not reply; he was shifting his gaze from one of their captives to the other. The full moon which had been hanging like a gibbous ghost in the darkening sky was beginning to glow now. Its shine was making the landscape almost as bright as day.

At last Longarm said, "Why, I ain't got no druthers, but I figure whichever one of these fellows I start cutting on just might decide to tell us what we're after. And for openers I'd as lief get myself started by just taking his fingers off one at a time."

"You still ain't said which one you want to carve up first," Callahan reminded him.

"It don't make much never-mind to me," Longarm replied. He'd slipped his sheath-knife out of its leather scabbard while Callahan was speaking. Running his thumb along the blade's edge and shaking his head, he said, "It needs to be edged up a mite, so it'll likely hurt more'n it generally does. But I don't aim to waste time just to accommodate a man who ain't got enough brains to keep his fingers where they oughta be."

"Then tell me which one of these rustlers you want to work on first," Callahan urged. "I'll hold him still while you carve him."

"I reckon we better start with the big one," Longarm replied. "The one that calls himself Parkins. I'm a little bit out of practice, and he looks like the easiest one of 'em to slice at. I'll get back in form by the time I've cut off a few of his fingers. If the big one ain't cracked his jaws after I work on him a while, we'll start on the other fellow and see if he's any smarter."

Callahan started toward Parkins. The bound man looked even larger than he actually was, with arms pinned to his sides by his bonds and his legs secured by overlapping turns of the lariat.

"Now, hold on here!" Parkins protested. "You don't really aim to cut my fingers off of me, do you? Damn it, that's a Redskin trick! It sure ain't the way one white man oughta treat one of his own kind!"

107

"A white man can learn a lot from Redskins," Longarm stated. "Where do you think I learned how to slice pieces off of somebody and do it so's they'd live long enough to answer some questions?"

"Hell, that's downright heathenish!" Fonzo said. There was a hollow sound to his voice, as though he knew that his protest meant nothing.

"Some folks might call it that," Longarm agreed. He was careful to keep his voice casual rather than threatening. He'd learned that outlaws who themselves lived by threats were more impressed by calm certainty. He went on. "But I've done it so many times it don't bother me much more than slicing off a piece of juicy roast beef to put on my supper plate."

As he spoke, Longarm was hunkering down beside Parkins. He passed the blade of his knife back and forth in front of the man's face to give him a close view of its sharp shining steel edge. Parkins turned his head as far as he could to one side to avoid looking at the weapon that he was convinced would soon be cutting into him.

Longarm went on. "Now, the first thing I like to do is take all the meat off of a man's hands, strip 'em right down to their bones, so's I can get to the joints easier. Then I slip my knife in them little cracks and cut right on down, one joint after the other."

While Longarm was talking he touched the point of his blade to the web at the base of the outlaw's thumb. He placed the tip of the blade at the point where the large arm vein formed a vee carrying a branch of the vein to the back of the hand.

"I ain't aiming to miss this joint," he said. He did not have to press his knife blade very hard to start a small thread of blood trickling down Parkins's hand and fingers. Then he went on. "Now, maybe you'd best grit your teeth to keep from yelling when I jab it in to chop through them little muscles you keep twitching."

Since Parkins had felt the sharp point of the knife blade touch his hand he'd been grinding his teeth together as he clamped his jaws closed. Now he gazed at the thin trickle of blood oozing from the small incision Longarm had made.

"Hold on, damn you!" he yelled suddenly. "I ain't going to give my fingers or my hand away to nobody! Go ahead and ask your questions! I'll tell you what you want to know!"

"Shut up, damn it!" Fonzo burst out. "Them fellows that's waiting for us will have our hides if we spill anything to these bastards!"

"And we'll have your hides if you don't!" Longarm snapped. "Now, make up your minds which way it's going to be!"

"You swear to God you won't go ahead and take off our fingers or maybe just kill us outright after we've told you what you're after?" Parsons asked.

"My word's good," Longarm assured the outlaw. "I don't need to do no swearing."

"He's telling you the truth," Callahan put in quickly. "And even if he ain't told you his name, maybe you'd like to know it. He's United States Marshal Custis Long. You might even've heard about him someplace."

"You're saying he's the one they call Longarm?" Fonzo asked, incredulity tingeing his voice.

"He's telling you the gospel truth," Longarm assured the outlaws. "If you don't believe him, I'll be right glad to haul out my badge and give you a look at it. And you'll save yourself a big lot of trouble if you do what I'm telling you to."

For a moment the bound man flicked his eyes from his outlaw companion to Longarm and Callahan. Defeat was in the sullen tone of Fonzo's voice as he returned his attention to Longarm and said, "Go on and ask me what you want to know."

"All I want to know is just two things," Longarm told him. "One is who you're working for. The other one is where we got to go to find him."

"Now, that's a pretty big order," the outlaw said. "But if you're who you say you are, likely you'll know more'n a little bit about the way the land lays here."

"Well, I don't know all that much," Longarm told him. "But I do know a little bit. Now, suppose you just go ahead and tell me what your boss outlaw's name is and where he's waiting for you to meet him."

"He calls hisself Struthers," Fonzo replied. "And unless he's already got tired of waiting, you'll find him about six miles to the south of here. There's a little pond there, where him and his men was supposed to wait for us to drive them steers to. A bigger herd's already gone ahead of us."

"Now you're talking the kind of language I can understand," Longarm told the prisoner. "But I reckon I'm going to need for you to tell me a mite more about where we need to be going and how many we can look for in the bunch we'll be running into."

"That's just the same as if you was pushing a gun up against my head with your finger on the trigger!" Fonzo protested. "If I told you what all you're asking about, Struthers'd cut me down like the cold-blooded bastard he is!"

"Well, you're going to jail along with Struthers, because I ain't bragging when I tell you I aim to catch up with him and arrest him," Longarm reminded Fonzo. "But if it's going to make you feel like telling us where I got to go to find him, I can fix things up so that you and him won't be in the same cell."

"Oh, he'd find a way to get at me if he had any idea I'd steered you to where you can find him," Fonzo replied.

"Damn it, I've seen Struthers shoot a saloon flunky that was emptying spittoons along the foot-trail just because the poor devil spilled a little bit of slop on his boots!"

"There ain't no reason for this Struthers to know that you men even seen us, let alone told us anything about him," Longarm reminded him.

"You don't know how that devil hears things, Marshal Long," Fonzo replied. "He's got folks around here buffaloed so bad that they don't even call his name unless they're saying yes to him, and then they got to remember to touch their hat brims."

Before Longarm could answer, Callahan said, "Maybe it'd be handier if we knew where Struthers was heading, but I don't see that it makes all that much difference. That bigger herd will leave enough trail for us to follow easy."

"Well, I'd've rather circled around to get in front of him," Longarm stated. "But what you said's right. Suppose we take out after that Struthers and see for sure what he's up to."

"Now, hold on a minute!" Fonzo protested. "What about us? You ain't aiming just to leave us here for the wolves and the coyotes, are you?"

"There ain't a wolf or coyote anyplace around that'd touch a rotten piece of meat like you," Longarm told the outlaw. "But we'll likely be back before they get at you enough to save us the trouble of carting you off to jail. Maybe you'll get lucky and your friend watching your herd will come back."

Callahan had already reined around and was starting to ride. Longarm followed him and caught up; then the two men rode side by side to pick up the broad hoof-pocked trail that had been left by the larger herd of stolen steers. During the time they'd spent dragging the information they needed from the two rustlers the moon's glow had increased its intensity to an almost daytime brilliance.

Though the distance was still shrouded a bit, nearby clumps of cactus and the contours of the upsloping terrain were clearly visible. On the light-hued golden yellow desert sand, the hoofmarks of cattle and horses could be distinguished quite readily. Longarm and Callahan had been in the saddle for less than an hour before they could see the sandy soil was beginning to darken. Ahead the terrain sloped gently upward in contrast to the flat featureless country they'd been riding over.

"If I ain't making a bad guess, we're back in the hill country," Longarm said as their mounts began to move a bit more slowly on the upslope they soon reached.

"I suppose," Callahan agreed. "Which means we'll be moving a little bit slower, because from here it looks like the going's not going to be quite as easy."

"Oh, I can see that," Longarm told his companion. "But we ain't lost the tracks of that cattle herd yet, and I ain't aiming to lose 'em now. We'll just have to keep a sharper look and maybe slow down a mite. If we can just catch up with 'em before daybreak, it's going to make our job a lot easier."

"You sure was right about us not losing no ground till we got into these hills," Longarm said as Callahan reined in beside him. "We just ain't making as good time as I figured we could. This uphill country's slowing us down."

"And those rustlers are really pushing that bunch of steers they stole," Callahan observed. "They're not wasting a minute, but it sure ain't hard to figure out why. They're in a hurry to hand over that rustled herd to whoever's waiting for it before we can catch up to 'em."

"You hit it in one shot," Longarm agreed. "We'll want to be right close to 'em when that handing-over's being done. Because if we can nab them rustlers and the bunch that's getting the steers all at the same time, it'll sure give us a boost in getting this hill country started to tame down. Let's push on now. The quicker we catch up, the faster our job's going to be finished."

Chapter 11

Longarm and Callahan had rested their mounts briefly each time they'd urged the tired animals up the steep side of one of the hills, and now as they reached the top of another upslope they stopped to survey the vista below them. Beyond a short level stretch in the valley between their present position and the next rise, the ragged terrain seemed to be leapfrogging ahead, to form an endless series of humps waiting for the animals to labor up their sharply sloping sides.

They hadn't caught up with the herd though they'd ridden all day. With the day now near its end, the horses had slowed greatly. While they'd mounted the rise to their present position in the expanse of rolling hills through which Longarm and Callahan were passing, the tiring animals had moved much more slowly and reluctantly than they had while mounting the earlier slopes.

"We still ain't seen nothing but steers' hoofprints lately," Callahan remarked. "If there was any horses that left prints, the cattle covered 'em. And if we don't catch up with them rustlers pretty soon, we ain't got much chance of seeing hide nor hair of that bunch they're driving."

"Trouble is, those rustlers up ahead had too big of a start on us," Longarm said.

Longarm was taking advantage of their rest stop to light up one of his long thin cigars. After he'd puffed its tip into a glowing coal and exhaled a cloud of blue-gray smoke he added, "But we're still holding to the trail they left, if that makes you feel any better."

"Well, it does and it don't," Callahan replied. "I'd a lot sooner catch up with that outfit in daylight instead of in the dark, and most of the day's already gone."

"You ain't just talking to yourself when you say that," Longarm told him.

Callahan went on. "I like to see what I'm aiming at instead of wasting good powder and lead shooting at nothing but muzzle flashes."

"Oh, I feel the same way," Longarm assured his companion. "But you got to admit that we ain't got no druthers. Right now we've got to move spry, because there's just the two of us and by the look of the cattle tracks we've spotted we'll be looking at maybe a half-dozen or more of them rustlers."

"A half-dozen's about enough for me."

"Oh, it is for me too," Longarm assured him. "But we oughta be able to even the odds, if we can work out a way to take 'em by surprise."

"You're saying that if we do catch up before sundown, we'd better wait for full dark before we jump 'em?"

"It's what I been thinking on," Longarm admitted. "But we got to catch up to 'em before we can really figure out what to do. Now, I'd say these horses don't need any more rest than they've already had. We better get back to business."

"If you're ready to go on ahead, I'm right with you," Callahan assured him.

Longarm touched his horse's barrel with his boot toe. The animal began moving, and Callahan set his own mount into motion. The slope they were starting to descend now was gentler than the one they'd just mounted. At its bottom a long flat stretch of rich grassland lay between them and the next rising ground, perhaps a dozen miles distant.

A crushed and trampled swath of high grass cutting through the lush grazing land in front of them marked with unmistakable clarity the path in which the rustled steers had been driven. By wordless mutual consent both men reined in to the center of the grass-trail. They rode in silence, closer together than before, glancing often at the western horizon. Its undulating line, which had been so clear-cut only a few minutes earlier, was now beginning to merge with the darkening sky, for the clear air was already taking on the dim obscurity that comes with nightfall.

"If them fellows up ahead don't stop pretty soon, they're in for a heap of trouble," Longarm remarked. "Steers don't move bunched up at night the way they do in daytime."

"Since I never have been a ranch hand, I wouldn't know a lot about that," Callahan said. "But I'm in favor of anything that might help us a little bit."

"Dark ain't going to help us find them much, that's certain-sure," Longarm told his companion. "Not unless them outlaws are fool enough to light a cooking fire."

"But we'd certainly be able to see it if they did," Callahan said.

Longarm shook his head. "That don't rightly follow. Even was they to build a fire, I doubt they'd light it anyplace but in the bottom of one of these little valleys, where the hills would hide it. And don't forget, there are a lot of caves in this hill country. There might be one hereabouts they could build up a good blaze in."

"You don't think we could hear the steers blatting?"

"Sure, we could, if we were close enough."

Longarm's reply might have been a stage cue spoken by an actor. He'd barely finished speaking when the flat nasal blat of a steer communicating with its fellows sounded through the constantly deepening dusk ahead of them. Even before it had died away the single call set off a half-dozen replies, and for several moments the still air was filled with sounds. Then, as the noisy steers quit blatting and their sounds faded into silence, Longarm and Callahan heard the scuffling thuds of horse hooves and the much fainter and unintelligible sounds of men's raised voices.

"Looks like we're close enough," Callahan observed.

"We're that, all right," Longarm agreed. "And while them rustlers are busy riding herd, let's us sneak up and take a close look at what's going on and see how the land lays, so we can figure out the best way to get at 'em."

They toed their mounts ahead. As close as they'd been to the crest of the rise when the blatting cattle cries had sounded, it took them only a few moments to ride within a dozen yards of its low rounded top. Longarm pulled up and Callahan reined in beside him.

"I figure we best get up the rest of the way to the top on shank's mare," Longarm said. "If we rode all the way up, that sky's still bright enough for them to be sure to spot us before we've had a good look at 'em."

"Makes sense," Callahan agreed. "We've been riding these nags long enough to know they'll stand."

Having learned earlier that they could depend on their livery mounts not to stray after a rider had dismounted, they wasted no time in leaving their saddles and dropping the reins of their horses to the ground. Longarm slid his rifle out of its saddle-scabbard and Callahan followed his example. Shifting the guns to their left hands, the two men started toward the crest of the gently rounded slope.

Ahead of them the grade of the small shelving hillock rose gently. They started for its rounded top, with Callahan letting Longarm set their pace. Even after their first saddle-stiffness had been worked off, he made it a slow, easy stride in order to create the smallest possible noises.

They moved steadily up the gentle grade, bending forward a bit from their waists to balance themselves on the slope. Within a very few minutes they were nearing the top of the rise. Longarm gestured for Callahan to stop.

"Belly-crawling ain't my favorite way of traveling," Longarm observed after they'd stood listening for a moment, scanning the crest that was now only a few paces away from them. "But that's how we'd best go till we get where we're headed."

Callahan acknowledged Longarm's suggestion with a nod, and both men dropped to their knees, then shifted their rifles to a left-hand carry as they leaned forward to begin crawling. They made only gentle rustling noises as they pushed through the tall grass that sheltered them. Even before they'd reached the crest of the little rise they could hear quite clearly the voices of the outlaws on the down-slope beyond.

"No, damn it!" one of the men beyond the rise was saying. "We don't move these steers another foot tonight! Nor tomorrow neither! This is where that bunch coming after 'em is supposed to meet us, and I'm not a big enough jackass to risk losing the wad of money they're bringing to pay for 'em. Anyways, you better be glad to wait for 'em, just like I am, because if I don't get paid, neither do you!"

"Just hold on for a minute!" one of the rustlers said.

"Every time it looks like we're getting someplace, you trot out a new story to hang us up. Now, you're saying we ain't got no choice but to stay here if we're going to draw down our share of the loot!"

"That's the way of it," the first speaker snapped. "Take it or leave it."

In the concealment of their hidden lookout, Callahan whispered to Longarm, "You got the same idea I did?"

"Sure," Longarm said. "If another bunch of outlaws joins up with this one, we'd be in a lot worse shape than now." He stopped to listen when another of the outlaws spoke.

"What about that girl at the hideout, Struthers?" a new voice called from the cluster of renegades. "When do you figure to hand out the ransom money we're supposed to split up?"

"Just like I told you, you'll get what's coming to you soon as her old man pays up to get her back," the leader replied.

"What if he don't pay?" the questioner persisted. "If her daddy don't pony up with the ransom, we'll end up with nothing."

"Oh, we can do better'n that," Struthers said confidently. "If we don't get ransom money we'll take her to Mamie Riley's whorehouse and see how much Mamie's willing to pay for her."

"Now, I might stand still for that," the man asking the questions said. "Provided we all get a free chance at her before we take her to Mamie's."

Longarm's wrath had been increasing steadily during the exchanges between the outlaws. Now he bent his head close to Callahan's and whispered, "I guess you read that the same as I do?"

"Sure. They got some poor little girl in that hideout they was talking about that they're figuring to sell and make a whore out of."

120

"Which means it's a sight more important to stop them bastards from doing that than it is to save a few head of rustled cattle."

"Maybe the outlaws wouldn't agree with you," Callahan said. "But I sure got to. Except that with just the two of us—"

"Never mind about that," Longarm broke in. "Whoever's buying the steers might show up in the next few minutes. There's no way to tell."

"You're saying we ought to move now?"

"I ain't saying it right out flat yet. All I'm doing is sorting things out."

"Let me know when you've got it sorted," Callahan suggested.

Longarm did not answer for a moment, and when he did speak his words came slowly and thoughtfully. "If we jump the rustlers now, we might lose the girl. You think on it a while longer, though, and you start wondering if we might not have better odds by moving in."

"Speaking as one gambling man to another, I got to agree with you."

"I figure we ought to be able to find out where their hideout is. After that, whichever way things work out, we can get the girl away from 'em."

Callahan thought for a moment. "That might be the best way."

Longarm nodded. "We can always pick up the trail this cattle herd's going to leave when it's sold, but the thing we need to do first of all is to find out where that girl is and get her outa their hands."

"I'm of a mind to back up your bet, because it won't be too long before it'll be too dark to see."

"With a little bit of luck to help us, if we move quick and hit hard, we might even be able to get her free and then circle back to give whoever's buying that herd a bigger surprise than they'd get out of a stampede."

"Sounds to me like we're about to be real busy, but I'll be satisfied to let you call the shots," Callahan said. "Just say the word and we'll get started."

Longarm turned away from his companion long enough to take another quick look at the herd of steers and the men clustered at the base of the slope where the cattle had been stopped. Then he turned back to Callahan.

"Look at how the rustlers are all bunched up down by the bottom of this rise, between it and the steers," he said, gesturing toward the outlaws as he spoke. "There ain't but five of 'em, and they're so busy jawing that they ain't paying no mind to much but themselves."

"You've got a plan worked up?"

"Maybe," Longarm answered. "Except that plans don't always work out the way a man figures they will. They'll be having to break away from their confab pretty quick to look after the steers. I figure when they bust up and scatter, we can pick out one of 'em without too much trouble."

"And make him lead us to their hideout?"

"Chances are that it ain't too far off, or they wouldn't've stopped here with the herd. If it ain't close, my idea ain't no good and we'll have to try something else. But right now let's try the first way. One of us can stay, and soon as we find out where their hideout is the other one can make a quick sneak for it. Whichever one of us stays behind can muss up their scheme to hand over the herd by keeping 'em busy here."

Callahan had been following Longarm's words and gestures. When he'd heard the plan he nodded. "It's risky, but I guess it's the best we can do. You got any druthers about going or staying?"

122

"Nary a one," Longarm replied. "Take your pick."

"Suppose I stay then, and you scout around. I'd guess you're better at that than I'd be," Callahan suggested. "You keep an eye on them as best you can while you're scouting, and give me a wave when you're ready for me to start shooting."

"Better'n that," Longarm said quickly. "It's getting dark fast. We can still see each other plain enough, but you might not be able to see me wave. Let's say I look your way every once in a while, and when I see you're in place, I'll let off the first shot, and that's the time for you to start shooting."

"That makes sense to me," Callahan said. "So let's get moving before it's too dark to see who we're shooting at."

Callahan was reining away even before Longarm could voice his agreement. Longarm returned his attention to the outlaws. While he and Callahan had been making their arrangements the rustlers had scattered.

Longarm made a quick decision. Shouldering his rifle, he picked the outlaw furthest apart from the others and squeezed off a shot. When the bullet went home the outlaw jerked back in his saddle and almost slipped off it, but managed to throw his torso forward and lie shielded behind the neck of his horse.

A rifle barked, and only Longarm's swiftness in following his adversary's example by dropping forward across the neck of his mount saved him from being the shooter's prey. Longarm slid the butt of his rifle between his thigh and saddle-skirt and reached back to draw his Colt. He had the weapon in his hand and was scanning the scattered outlaw band when a yell from Callahan reached his ears.

"Longarm! Back of you!" Callahan shouted.

Somehow, Longarm managed to toe his horse and force it to turn without having to grasp the reins in his gun hand. Despite the handicap of being forced to hold his awkward position, he was lifting his Colt while the horse was turning. He saw at once that he had a target made to order, an outlaw galloping toward him, raising his revolver.

Longarm risked breaking the slanting sidewise stance in which he was clinging. He began straightening up while lifting his Colt from its awkward angle. He tightened the grip of his left hand on the reins and swung his gun hand, thumbing the pistol's hammer back as he brought its muzzle around. An instant of flip-cock aim was all that he had time for before firing.

In spite of the hurried and awkward stance, Longarm's lead went true again. The outlaw's arm dropped and the fingers which had been clenched around his revolver's butt relaxed as he was thrown back in his saddle by the impact of Longarm's bullet. The pistol dropped, then slid from the outlaw's hand as he toppled from his saddle and sprawled motionless on the ground.

Two quick gunshots barking from Callahan's direction broke the already roiled air. Longarm glanced around, looking for his companion, and finally caught sight of him through the haze of gunsmoke that was now shimmering in puffs and pillars as it rose to dissipate in the still air.

While Longarm had been scanning the area in search of Callahan he'd noticed that the herd beyond the area of the gunfight was beginning to move restlessly. Standing up in his stirrups and raising his arm, Longarm waved it in a circle two or three times before attracting Callahan's attention. When he saw his companion looking at him, he pointed toward the section of the herd which was in greatest disarray.

Waiting until Callahan had wheeled his horse and started toward the troubled area, Longarm nudged his mount into motion and set out to learn whether their sketchy improvised plan might have a chance of working.

Chapter 12

Longarm reined his mount on a zigzag course to avoid the clumped cattle that formed the most active areas of the stretch of prairie over which the milling herd was scattered. The descending sun was low enough now to shine in his eyes when he cocked his head sidewise or tilted it back. Now and then he halted the horse and levered himself up to stand in the saddle, using his rifle as a tightrope walker might use a staff to balance his unsteady footing while he scanned the area around him, looking for Callahan. The rustlers were scattering now, running away from the suddenly restless herd.

At last Callahan came into Longarm's field of vision. He was riding the same pattern that Longarm had followed, zigzagging back and forth as he guided his horse through the small clumps of milling steers. A glance told Longarm that Callahan needed no help, but nevertheless he looked back now and then.

Picking his way, dodging when needed, Longarm had gotten almost all the way through the small clumped groups and the aimlessly wandering loners of the herd. The animals had spread out widely after the herd had broken up, but at last Longarm got almost to the edge of the still-milling herd and saw a saddled but riderless horse. Reining toward it, Longarm soon saw the figure of one of the outlaws lying near the horse.

Longarm was still some distance away when the sprawled outlaw stirred and slowly struggled to a sitting position. Longarm could see that the man was wounded, for he had his left arm across his chest, its hand clamped over the biceps of his right arm. As Longarm drew closer, the outlaw saw him and dropped his right hand to his hip, clawing clumsily for the butt of his revolver.

"Don't do it!" Longarm called, raising the rifle. "I ain't one for shooting a hurt man in cold blood, but if you get hold of that six-gun you're reaching for, that's when I trigger down on you!"

For a moment the wounded outlaw hesitated. Then he let his reaching hand drop and raised his other arm above his head as he said, "I ain't fool enough to ask for a bullet, mister. I'll take a while in jail instead. You and me's strangers, but by the way you talk, I reckon you're the law?"

"You reckoned right," Longarm replied. He kept his rifle pointed in the direction of the outlaw, but did not draw a bead on the recumbent man as he went on. "But don't look for me to waste no time getting you to a jail."

"Now, wait a damned minute!" the outlaw exclaimed. "You said you wouldn't shoot me in cold blood!"

"Why, that'll depend on you," Longarm told the rustler. "It'd save a lot of time and trouble if I did pull a trigger on you, but from the way you look you just might be smart enough to get yourself a trial up in front of a judge and jury."

"Look, mister, I ain't rolling in money, or I wouldn't be mixed up in this mess," the outlaw protested. "I maybe could scrape up enough to toss on the bar was I buying you a drink, but that's about the size of it."

"You took what I said wrong," Longarm told him. "I ain't after money. I want information."

"What makes you figure I got any?" the outlaw demanded. "I ain't bossing this bunch."

"Maybe you better tell me who is," Longarm suggested.

"Names don't mean much when you're on the wrong side of the law," the rustler said, managing a lopsided grimace that could have passsed for a grin. "I've got three or four I travel under, and the boss of this outfit—well, I've heard him answer to Gregory and Simmons and two or three more."

"How about Struthers?" Longarm asked.

"Oh, sure. Struthers or Druthers or something like that."

"Well, now," Longarm said. "Since you've got started talking, maybe you can tell me where your boss hangs out when he's in this part of the hill country. I figure if this is where all the rustled steers is sold, he'd likely have a place somewhere close by."

For a long moment the outlaw did not answer. Then he asked, "What's in it for me if I tell you?"

"I ain't buying nothing, if that's what you got in mind," Longarm replied. "And I ain't got time to waste. If you don't talk I'll give you a dose of lead and find somebody else that will. But if I know where to find the place your boss stays at, I might just let you alone right now and go looking for it."

This time the outlaw did not reply at once, as he had when answering Longarm's earlier questions. Though Longarm wanted to turn and look at the area where the rustled cattle were located to see how Callahan was doing, he resisted the temptation. The noises from the herd had diminished. There was no shooting now, only the distant thud of horses' hooves and the blatting of the milling steers.

Satisfied that Callahan needed no help at the moment,

Longarm kept his attention focused on the outlaw, who'd stayed almost totally motionless. The man's face was twisted, either in pain from the wound he was nursing or from agonized thought, but before Longarm could speak the prisoner replied with a question of his own.

"How do I know you won't just finish me off after I've told you what you're after?"

"Because I told you I wouldn't," Longarm told him. "And you can take that for the best offer I aim to make."

There was a finality in Longarm's tone as he spoke, and while he'd been delivering his ultimatum he was also raising the barrel of his rifle until the rustler's eyes were only inches from its muzzle. Now the reply he'd been anticipating came promptly.

"He's got him a little shanty a ways up this draw," the man said. "It ain't hard to find, just go through that cut over yonder and keep moving up the valley till you see it."

Longarm studied the area which the outlaw had indicated. At first he could not make out anything except the gradual rise of the ridge that rose above the mouth of a small valley between him and the skyline. Then his keen vision, added to years of chasing criminals over strange stretches of land, came to his assistance. The valley was not a rocky gulch, but a wide grassy depression; it was the sort of place where even a makeshift cabin would be protected from the winter's worst storms.

"How much of a ride is it to that shanty you told me about?" Longarm asked.

"Maybe a little bit under half an hour, say twenty minutes."

"I reckon that's what I'll settle for then," Longarm told the man. He raised the rifle's muzzle again.

"Hold on now! You said you wasn't going to shoot me!" the outlaw protested.

"And I don't aim to," Longarm assured him. "But I ain't going to give you no kind of chance to throw down on me. Now, just move slow and easy. Reach your left hand across your belly button till you can pull that six-gun outa your holster. Then you hold it by the butt with your thumb and two fingers and make sure the muzzle's pointing down."

Moving with slow reluctance, keeping his eyes fixed on Longarm, the outlaw lifted his revolver from its holster. He held it by the grip in front of his midsection, barrel down, waiting for Longarm to give him additional instructions.

"You're doing good so far," Longarm said. He nodded to indicate a good-sized expanse of gravel ten or fifteen feet distant. The small white stones supported several small clumps of struggling pale-green grass. Longarm went on. "Now, just swing your arm and toss that six-gun over by them little bunches of grass yonder."

Although the outlaw's slow movements were further evidence of his reluctance, he obeyed Longarm's command and swung his arm to send the revolver sailing in a low arc through the air. It landed with a scraping thunk on the gravel.

"Now get on outa here!" Longarm snapped. "You'll find a bunch from your outfit after you get out on the prairie, and I'd imagine the fellow that's with me'll be keeping 'em corraled with a rifle. If you start running, don't be surprised if he cuts you down. If you just mind your p's and q's you might come outa this without no holes in your hide."

With a quick nod of understanding the outlaw started walking toward the end of the gully. Longarm watched him for a moment, until he disappeared around a bulge in the depression's cleft, then rode forward into the shallow valley. He'd ridden for only a short distance when he saw what he'd been looking for, a small dilapidated cabin nestled close to the base of a high flat-faced boulder that dwarfed the structure it was helping to support.

"Looks like you found the place you been looking for, old son," he said, his voice loud in the still air. After he'd continued his study of the little building for a few moments longer he shook his head. "It sure ain't nothing like the Brown Palace Hotel, but it's the only place you've run into. Now, there ain't no horses anyplace around, so that makes it a pretty safe bet there ain't nobody waiting to potshot you. That being the way of it, you'd best go and see if there just might not be somebody else in that little shanty."

Toeing his horse into motion, Longarm advanced slowly toward the ramshackle structure. Drawing closer, he could see that the door opened outward and was partly ajar, hanging crookedly by a single hinge near its center. Raising the muzzle of his rifle to cover the doorway, he pulled up a short distance from the ramshackle cabin.

"Anybody in there?" he called.

When no answer to his question came from the door, he slid his Winchester into its saddle scabbard and dismounted. Then he began walking toward the door of the cabin. As he drew close to it, Longarm heard a strange muffled metallic noise coming from the interior. Taking no chances, he drew his Colt and stepped to one side of the dangling door before resuming his slow advance.

By the time Longarm had changed the angle of his approach the odd sounds coming from the cabin had stopped. Then after a moment they started again. When he tried to peer through the partly opened doorway the only thing he could see with any clarity through the half-dark that shrouded the small visible portion of the interior was the corner of a table.

"Whoever you are in there, you'd best talk to me, or I'll be coming in shooting!" Longarm called. He waited, but no response came from the shack's darkened interior. He waited for a moment, then muttered to himself in a half-whisper, "Old son, you're damned if you do and you're damned if you don't. All you can do is give it a try and whatever happens, be ready to do what you need to."

Stepping a bit to one side, he raised his revolver. Then he lifted the foot nearest the doorway and gave the dangling door a hard kick. There was a crack of splintering wood and a small screeching as the bottom edge of the door scraped the cabin's floor while opening wider. Longarm dived inside, his Colt ready in his hand, and rolled into a half-crouch.

Longarm rolled across the scanty expanse of floor until he was stopped by the legs of two chairs and a table. He levered himself to his knees, his Colt raised, and glanced around the small room.

For a moment the dusky gloom inside the cabin's cramped interior hindered Longarm's vision. Then on the far side of the small room, half-hidden by the open door, he saw a bed and a naked woman lying on it. She was lashed to the bed by ropes that held her upraised wrists to its headboard of brass rods and her outspread ankles were tied in similar fashion to the bedstead's foot. A strip of folded cloth was wrapped around her mouth, and she was staring at Longarm, her eyes opened wide, her throat gurgling with the words she was unable to form.

Taken totally aback by the unexpected scene in the cramped cabin, Longarm looked at the bound woman for several moments, then flicked his eyes quickly around the single room's interior. The bed, a deal table against the opposite side of the windowless room, and a small scattering of four or five chairs were its most visible contents. He also saw a large wooden box under the table, and nails or pegs on the back wall that held a scanty array of indiscriminate garments: a pair of pants, two or three shirts, and an oilskin slicker.

133

"I'll get you freed up soon as I can fish out my knife," Longarm told the woman as he reached into his trousers pocket for his clasp-knife.

A gargle of unintelligible noises came from the woman's bound mouth. Longarm started toward the bedside, opening the knife's biggest blade as he moved. She jerked convulsively as she saw the glint of the well-honed blade's steel, and Longarm stopped before reaching the bed.

"Now, I ain't here to hurt you none," he said reassuringly. "I ain't one of the rustlers. My name's Long, Custis Long. I'm a deputy United States marshal, outa the Denver office, so if you live hereabouts you wouldn't know me. But you got to hold real still right now while I'm cutting the ropes, or you might hurt yourself. And soon as I get your arms and legs free, I'll get rid of that gag for you."

Before Longarm had finished speaking the woman on the bed was visibly relaxing. She lay quietly while he carefully cut away the ropes that had held her hands and feet to the bed. Then, when Longarm moved to the side of the bed to cut away the gag that had enforced her silence, she inhaled deeply for a moment, drawing a free flow of fresh air into her lungs before she let him raise her to sit on the bedside.

"I'm Margaret Wells," she said after she'd stopped her deep gasping inhalations. "And if you're a United States marshal, it's likely you've heard of my grandfather. He was the first U.S. chief marshal here in Texas after it came into the Union."

"You don't need to say no more," Longarm assured her. He tried to keep his eyes away from the pebbled tips of her bared breasts and the total nudity of her body. "There ain't a marshal on the force that don't know about Chief Marshal Coy Barrett, and how he helped the Rangers clean up Texas."

"I think one reason the outlaws were interested in me at first was because of him," she said. "But that didn't stop them from . . ." Breaking off suddenly, she indicated the bed and the ropes dangling from it.

Longarm spoke quickly. "Stands to reason that those outlaws had you tied up here on account of they figured to get ransom for you."

"That's quite probably why I'm still alive," she said. "But the outlaws have . . ." She stopped short and shook her head as she went on. "I don't suppose I need to give you chapter and verse. All I'll say is that it's been something I don't ever want to go through again."

"We still ain't what you'd call outa the woods," Longarm reminded her. "But we better get busy and find you some clothes. I ain't sure how long Callahan can keep those outlaws busy."

"You're not by yourself then?"

"Right now, I might as well be," he told her. "But my partner on this case ain't too far away. I guess your clothes are someplace in here, Miss Margaret?"

"I'm afraid not. The outlaws . . ." Stopping short, she shook her head. "They stripped me and slashed my clothes to rags with their knives. They said I wasn't going to need them any longer, that I'd be—well, the only polite way to put it is that I'd be dead before they left."

"You just sit still, I'll see what I can rummage out," Longarm told her.

He looked around the cabin's bare interior, then pulled out the box that was under the table. Some pieces of cloth covered the box's contents, and when Longarm lifted the fabric it unfolded to reveal that it was a dress. Glancing into the box, Longarm saw no more clothing, only a scattering of revolver holsters and heaps of ammunition boxes. Straightening up, he handed the garment to Margaret.

"I don't know as how you can get into this," he said. "But it's all I found in there."

"And it happens to be the dress those outlaws stripped off me," Margaret said. "They tore up all my underclothes, slashed my boots to ribbons, and—well, I won't go on. Toss me the dress, please, Marshal Long. It'll do me until I can find something else to wear."

Longarm turned his back while Margaret was slipping into the dress. For lack of anything else to do, he glanced into the box of shells again. A familiar outline caught his eyes. He hunkered down beside the box and scrabbled through the litter of loose ammunition until his fingertips touched leather. He dug for a moment before uncovering a scarred and battered pair of boots. When he lifted them out one at a time, the second boot weighed much heavier than the first, and in it he discovered a battered Colt revolver.

Although the weapon was old, its blueing rubbed away from both the cylinder and the barrel, it still shone with gun oil. Longarm pulled the hammer to half-cock and twirled the cylinder. It moved easily, and when he swung the cylinder out Longarm saw that it had a load in every chamber.

Without waiting to paw through the remaining shells on the bottom of the box, Longarm stood up and extended the boots and the weapon to Margaret. He said, "I got lucky. Likely you can make these boots do you till we get where we'll be heading, and I reckon you'd know how to pull a trigger, so here's a gun for you. It's old, but I reckon it might come in handy if you'd like to take it along."

"I certainly would!" she exclaimed. "And it just happens that I learned to shoot with a Colt just like it, one of Grand-dad's old pistols."

"Then we best move out," Longarm said. "It's not a far piece to where we're heading, but I had to leave my partner on this case back there by himself, and he might need some help. The sooner we get back to where he is, the better it'll be for all of us."

Chapter 13

"How on earth did you manage to find me in that nasty little cabin that's so far away from anywhere?" Margaret Wells asked Longarm.

They had left the shack and were moving away from it, Longarm leading the way, heading toward his horse. He replied, "Why, it wasn't all that much of a job, Miss Margaret. Me and my partner—"

"Please," she said. "I hate to interrupt you, but do call me Meg. I'm so used to my nickname that I answer to it faster than I do to my full name."

"Sure, I can see how that'd be," Longarm said. "Maybe it's on account of I got a nickname too."

"And like I've told you, I've heard about you ever since I was a little girl!" she exclaimed. "From my grandfather, more than anybody else. He seems to remember the name of every law officer in the nation."

"And there still ain't enough of us to corral all the crooks and killers. But this kinda talk ain't what we oughta be wasting time on," he said. Then without allowing Margaret time to speak, he went on. "You were wondering how I come to find you. It wasn't on account of us looking for you."

"You mean you just stumbled on this cabin by accident?"

"I reckon that's about as close as you could come," Longarm agreed. "It's right one way, but it's wrong another way."

"It can't be both," she protested.

"Maybe not, but it is," he replied. "Me and the fellow that's with me were trailing some outlaws driving a herd of steers they rustled. We kept close as we could to 'em, and when they stopped the herd we snuck up closer, to hear what they were talking about. The first thing one of 'em said was that they had a girl held for ransom at their hideout. So I got one of outlaws alone and made him tell me where the hideout was."

"And you knew I was in the cabin?"

"Well, I figured you were," he replied. "But I also figured that if their boss had a cabin close by, he might stop off at it to pick up some loot he'd stashed away. He's the one we're hardest after."

"You're talking about Struthers?" Meg asked.

"If that's the name he's traveling under here," Longarm said. "But I'd bet a dollar to a plugged-up dime he's got some other names I could hang onto him."

Meg went on. "You missed him by—well, I'd say almost a half hour. He came hurrying in, grabbed his saddlebags off the wall where they were hanging, and left in as much of a hurry as he'd been when he got there. He barely looked at me, but I could tell something had gone wrong and he was trying to get away from whatever it was."

"What'd gone wrong was that me and my partner attacked his gang. We got other business to settle, but right now

I'd sure like to catch up with the boss of that rustler gang. I don't reckon you'd know which way he was heading?"

Meg thought for a moment, then said, "I wouldn't want to misdirect you, Mar—Longarm, but the best I can do is offer a guess."

"There's times when a guess is all I need," Longarm told her. "Maybe this'll be one of 'em."

"All I have to go by is how his horse's hoofbeats sounded," she went on. "I'm pretty sure he headed southeast."

They'd reached Longarm's horse by now. "Let's just tuck away that gun and stuff in my saddlebags. Then you can hold on easier."

Stowing the Colt away took only a moment. Longarm swung into his saddle and leaned down to extend a hand to Meg. She grasped it with the easy skill of a competent horsewoman, then as Longarm brought his arm up, she twisted as she was swinging in midair to place herself on the horse's rump behind him. Longarm nudged the animal with his boot toe and reined it toward where he'd left Callahan. He waited until the horse was moving steadily ahead before half-turning to his companion.

"You live hereabouts," he said. "So you'd know where there's towns to the southeast. It'll likely save me a lot of time if you can tell me about 'em. I sure need to figure out which one of 'em Struthers is most likely to be heading for."

"There aren't any towns really close to where we are now," she replied. "The nearest is to the west, beyond our family's spread. It's called Spring Branch, but I'd say there's no more than a dozen or so families in it. Then there's Fischer and Wimberly to the north. They're little places, not much bigger than Spring Branch. The big town's to the east, it's San Marcos."

"If you were making a bet with me where we'd be most apt to catch up with Struthers, which one would you pick out?" Longarm asked.

"My guess may be wrong, but I'd say that he's most likely to be heading for San Marcos. It's really the only town big enough for him to hide out in."

"How close'd that be from where we are now?"

"A little better than a day's ride. And I'm not saying that I'm guessing right, any more than I'd say I favor it because my grandfather's ranch is just this side of San Marcos."

"Were you anyplace close to it when those outlaws nabbed you?"

"I was almost midway from our own place to Granddad's. I was going to pay him a visit."

"Except you never got there."

"Halfway's about the best I managed," Meg said. "That's when the cattle herd crossed the trail I was on. Of course, it just didn't occur to me that there might be outlaws driving the steers. I started around to the back of the herd and one of the hands came riding toward me. I didn't think of him being a rustler or an outlaw until he pulled up by me and stuck a gun in my face. And you already know what happened after that."

"Now, the best thing you can do is get that part of what happened outa your mind," Longarm told her.

"I'm trying to, Longarm, but it's not something that most women can forget easily, especially so soon."

"Well, you work on it anyhow. Now, let's get back to what we were talking about. Is the Guadalupe the only real river hereabouts?"

"Well, there are a lot of little creeks that start from springs around here, but I guess you'd be right, calling the Guadalupe the only real river. A few of the creeks

142

flow into the Guadalupe, but most of the little ones just peter out or end up in mud flats. But there are some little towns along the river, and Struthers could be heading for one of them."

"I aim to get him, and I need to be taking out after him," Longarm told her. "But first I got to ride back to where me and my partner were swapping shots with those rustlers and see what's happened to him."

"You'll be going right near to where I live then," she said. "You will take me with you, I hope."

"Why, for certain-sure," Longarm assured her. "That was just a little gunfight back where my partner is, or I wouldn't've left him. I'd imagine there'll be a stray saddle horse or two around where the fracas began, because those rustlers had already lost the fight before I left."

"And I won't be in the way if you let me ride with you and your partner?"

Longarm noticed the quavery undertone in Meg's voice and hastened to reassure her. "Now, don't you start to worrying, because I sure didn't mean to upset you. Going with us is the best thing you can do, especially if it takes you close to home."

"I certainly don't mind going a little bit out of my way if it means that I'll be in safe company most of the time."

"I'll guarantee you that," Longarm told her.

"Well, I'm certainly glad you're not in too big a hurry to take me with you."

"Just don't worry no more. But if we were to run into any of those rustlers, I might have a little bit more shooting to do."

"Don't forget, I've got a gun now too. And I'm not a bad shot. Grandpa started teaching me—well, almost as long ago as I can remember. But I hope you don't mind if I steady myself by holding on to your belt."

"Grab on and welcome," Longarm replied as he toed the horse ahead. "And don't worry, I ain't going to run no race back to where I left Callahan."

There were no sounds of gunfire or any other disturbance other than the occasional blatt of a steer as Longarm and Margaret Wells drew closer to the area where Longarm and Callahan had first encountered the rustlers. The only sign that the cattle thieves had been busy were the straying steers that dotted the area. Some were loosely bunched in groups of three or four, but most of them had become loners and were grazing placidly by themselves, as though shunning their fellows.

True to Longarm's prediction, there were two saddled horses mingling with the steers, and at the edge of the area which they occupied, a blanket outlined the recumbent form of a dead body. Callahan had seen Longarm and Meg approaching and was weaving in and out among the widely spaced-out steers, riding to meet them. Longarm reined in to wait for him.

Turning to Meg, Longarm said, "That's Callahan, the fellow I told you about. And it looks like the shooting's over for a while. If there were any more live rustlers hereabouts, he wouldn't be lallygagging around waiting for us, he'd be out after 'em."

"I'm glad to see that the outlaws didn't kill him," she said. "They're about as mean a bunch of men as I've ever run into. I felt like—"

Longarm broke in to say, "Now don't go talking about what's over and done with. And don't think about it either. I ain't saying I know exactly how you feel, but the quicker you get it outa your mind, the better off you'll be."

Callahan was within hailing distance now. He called to

Longarm. "Those rustlers started scattering out right after you left. I got one of 'em, knocked him off his horse with a rifle shot, but that was the best I could do. He's laying over there with a blanket over him."

"I'd say you did a good job," Longarm called back. "I sure did hate to leave, but I had a pretty strong hunch you'd take care of yourself."

Longarm had not slowed his horse's gait, and within a few moments they could hold their voices to a conversational level rather than shouting. As Longarm reined he asked, "You mean the only rustler that's left here is that one you took early on?"

"That's the size of it," Callahan agreed. "Unless this young lady you brought back with you can give us some kind of idea about where they might be heading, we're just about down to starting out to look for 'em all over again."

"I already talked to her a little bit, but maybe you're righter than you figure when you said she might help us," Longarm said. "Her or her grandpa. I ain't had a chance to introduce you proper, but her name's Margaret Wells, and her grandpa's Coy Barrett."

"That's our Coy Barrett?" Callahan asked.

"There ain't but one of 'em that I know of," Longarm replied. "And from what Miss Margaret tells me, he's still spry as a spring chicken."

Meg broke in before Callahan could speak again. "He certainly is. And even if he's not a young man any longer, he knows more about the outlaws and bad men around here than most lawmen will ever learn."

"Well, I sure wouldn't argue that with you, ma'am," Callahan said soothingly. "And I'm right glad to meet you, Miss Margaret. Maybe it's not any of my business, but I'm wondering how you let the rustlers get their hands on you."

Longarm spoke before Meg could answer Callahan's question. "Now, that can wait, Cal. There'll be time to palaver later on, right now we got to get moving. Somebody's got to come out here and gather these steers, and I don't guess they'll scatter too bad once we got 'em bunched. We'll just have to leave 'em after we bunch 'em. Going after those outlaws that were driving 'em here is more important right now."

"Where'll we be looking then?" Callahan asked. He put the question to Longarm without looking at him. His eyes were studying Meg.

"Why, I figure we'll be getting some leads outa Coy Barrett, when we take his granddaughter home," Longarm answered.

"We could always use some help," Callahan said. "And maybe it'll get our case closed up a mite faster. But where are we going to head for first?"

"Well, San Marcos is the nearest town of any size nearby," Longarm replied. "Meg's home place is on the way there. Chief Barrett's spread's close by, and I'd sure like to visit with him a little while. From what I've heard, he knows chapter and book about these parts. And there's one or two other things that's popped into my mind. We know those rustlers had one big reason to stop here. To meet whoever was going to buy that herd of steers."

"Oh, I don't believe any of our neighbors would even think of buying a herd of stolen cattle!" Meg exclaimed.

"Maybe not," Longarm told her. "But there's some folks that're just naturally greedy. They don't ask too many questions when they're striking a bargain. And cattle brands can be changed real easy with a running iron. I got a hunch your grandpa might give us a few ideas, if we were to ask him. So let's just head for your home place, and see what we can find out about how the land lays. Maybe after I have a talk with your grandpa he can set me and Callahan on a fresh trail."

"We don't have very much further to go," Meg told Longarm and Callahan as they reined in at the edge of the riverbank. "This is the Blanco River, and San Marcos is only about ten more miles from here."

"Now, that's the best news I've heard since we started out," Longarm said. He gestured toward the greenish surface of the water where it was broken by large patches of a deeper green as he added, "Even if it does look sorta funny."

"All those dark places are over deep water," Meg explained. "Just go around them and you'll be all right. This river has its own quirks, and one of them is those sinkholes."

"We'll look out for 'em," Longarm said. "But me and Callahan's forded bigger rivers than this one, and I reckon you have too. Let's just get across it and be on our way."

"Perhaps I'd better lead you," she suggested. "I've forded the Blanco River more times than I can count."

"You're sure that's what you want to do?" Longarm asked. "You being on a nag you never saw till a little while ago?"

"Well, I've been riding him without any trouble since we left the herd," she replied. "This is just one time more."

Meg's last few words were spoken over her shoulder as she toed her horse into the stream. Longarm and Callahan kept their eyes fixed on her as the river's currents flowing around her mount's legs formed small frothy bubbles on its surface. Her progress was smooth until she was halfway across. Then they saw huge bubbles rise in big ripples against the horse's legs as the animal broke stride and started toppling to one side.

147

For a moment the horse struggled to hold its place in the center of the river. Then it neighed shrilly and its head went under, while Meg disappeared completely in the sudden roiling of froth that formed on the stream's surface.

Chapter 14

No words were needed between Longarm and Callahan when they saw Meg's head vanish under the rippling surface of the roiled water. As one man, they drummed their boot heels against their horses' flanks and reined the animals into the stream. By this time the water's surface was covered with small bursts of bubbles raised by the thrashing legs of the horse Meg had been riding. The riderless animal was still struggling to find solid bottom on which to plant its hooves, and its erratic movements were unpredictable.

At almost the same moment both Longarm and Callahan saw Meg's head rise from one of the bubble-blotched stretches of the river. Somehow her horse or a powerful underwater current had carried her almost to its center, and her arms were splashing as she fought the dragging water. The men tugged at the reins of their mounts, but the animals did not respond as they would have if they'd been on solid ground.

"Get downriver from her," Longarm called to Callahan. "I'll try to make it to her from here!"

A wave from Callahan acknowledged Longarm's shout. Then he saw Callahan turning to follow the stream's flow. By this time, Longarm's horse was slowly adjusting to its new, strange environment. He could feel its legs churning against the underwater current, and though he gripped the reins strongly, trying to guide the animal, his hands kept sliding along the wet slick leathers. He glanced at Meg, and saw that she'd begun trying to swim toward him and Callahan.

He also saw that Callahan was having the same trouble that he was experiencing. Longarm's horse was swimming, but when he tried to guide the animal he could not keep his hands from slipping on the wet leather of the reins. He looped them around his forearms, and the extra friction provided by the fabric of his shirtsleeves kept the reins from sliding so readily.

For the first time since hitting the water Longarm now felt that he had some semblance of control over his horse. It continued to churn its legs under the surface, but now it also responded to the familiar pressures of its reins. Carefully, still keeping a light touch on the leathers, Longarm managed to lean forward, stretching one arm toward Meg.

Though there was still a gap between them, Meg somehow managed to reach Longarm's extended hand. She locked her fingers around his wrist and clung, holding tightly, while Longarm leaned back in the saddle. Once she was near enough to span the short remaining distance, she grabbed his saddlehorn while Longarm leaned back as far as possible and raised his arm to help her.

With Longarm's grip to stabilize her, Meg could now slide her leg across him, and she bent the calf of her leg to pull herself closer. She was close enough now to allow Longarm to slip a hand under her armpit. He lifted her and tugged while she continued to lever herself high enough to slide down into the scant space between his thighs and the saddlehorn.

"I know you can't set like you're used to," Longarm told her. "But we'll manage to get on the bank this way."

"Anything to get out of this river," Meg replied. Her voice was as calm as though they were exchanging idle chatter at the dinner table. "As long as we're halfway across, we might as well go to shore on the side we started for. After we get on dry land, we'll just have a little way to go to get to Grandpa's spread."

"And we can't get all the way across too quick to suit me," Callahan told them as he finally reached the spot where Longarm's mount was beginning to struggle toward the shore.

"If we can get all the way across this pesky river before the current carries us too far, we won't have any trouble getting on the shore," Meg said. She pointed toward a short portion of the bank where its surface was almost level with that of the river. Beyond the low bank a cluster of huisache trees stretched for a quarter of a mile or more. "And those trees will cut the wind. We're going to be really cold when it hits us after we first get on land."

"Looks like all I got to do is keep tugging at these reins," Longarm said. "They're slicker'n the path to the devil's door, but I'll do the best I can."

He kept sawing at the reins as best he could, and the closer they got to the shoreline the harder he pulled to swing the horse in the direction of the trees. Somehow the horse got into the shallow water at the edge of the gently sloping bank. There the current was not as strong as it had been in midstream, and the tiring animal managed to struggle ashore. Its hooves slipped for a moment or two as it flailed its forefeet trying to lift itself and its human load out of the water; then its hooves plunged through the soft mud and found solid footing.

Callahan's lighter-loaded mount was just reaching the shoreline's shallows. It had less trouble getting all four of its hooves planted firmly and Callahan slid from the saddle. Still grasping the horse's reins, he waded in the ankle-deep water toward Longarm's horse and got his free hand into the head strap of its halter. Then he backed slowly up the little stretch of slippery riverbank mud, leading the horse bearing Longarm and Meg to dry ground.

"This Blanco River don't look so little to me any longer," Callahan remarked as he looked back at the stream. He took Meg's extended hand and helped her to the ground. Then he began swinging his legs one at a time to shake the water from them. "I know I'd sure hate to have to cross it more'n once like we just did. I hope there's not any more rivers between here and where we're heading."

"Don't worry," Meg assured him. "There's not even a brook between here and Grandpa's place."

"Now, that's the kind of talk I like to hear," Longarm said. He turned to Callahan. "I'd imagine the crossing was rougher on the horses than it was on us, but they'll get over their shakes real fast." Then he switched his attention to Margaret. "How much more of a ride is it to your grandpa's place?"

"It's not very far, only a little bit more than a mile after we get up to level land again," she replied. She gestured toward the gentle up-slope beyond the riverbank. "You'll be able to see his house just after we get to the top there."

"Well, then let's run down your horse and start moving again," Longarm suggested. "On account of we'll dry off faster when we ain't standing still, and we sure ain't going to get no place just staying around here wagging our jaws."

● ● ●

"Now, keep your eyes on that big chinaberry tree," Meg told her companions. They were riding abreast on the narrow dirt road, keeping their horses at a walk. Twisting in her saddle, she pointed toward a fluff of green darker than the hue of the thick-growing grass that sprouted on each side of the uphill road. "And in a minute you'll see the roof of Grandpa's house just beyond it."

Meg's minute passed swiftly. When they could see the straight line of a shingled roof beyond the tree, Longarm turned to her. "I don't reckon there'll be a chance he's not at home?"

"Grandpa doesn't leave home very often," she replied. "It's a wonder to me that he gets around as well as he does when he's bossing the help on his farm."

"Well, from what I've heard about your grandpa, he's a real tough gent," Longarm said. "He sure settled things down in a hurry when the muckety-mucks back in Washington put him in as chief marshal here in Texas."

"He doesn't talk much about the early years when he was . . ." Meg stopped as they neared the crest of the rise they'd been mounting. She pointed toward the outline which had suddenly appeared on the skyline ahead. "There's Grandpa's house now. We'll be there in just a few minutes."

When they topped the rise, the white two-story house ahead and the neat rows of growing green beyond it were plainly visible. Margaret toed her horse into a faster walk, and Longarm and Callahan nudged their mounts into a matching gait. They'd gotten to within a hundred yards of the house when a man dressed in summer whites appeared around a corner of the dwelling. He walked slowly, leaning on a cane, and stopped at the open double gate that broke the line of the barbed-wire fence.

"That's Grandpa," Meg said, waving her arm in greeting as she spoke.

She spurred ahead of Longarm and Callahan as the man returned her wave. By the time they'd reached her, she'd dismounted and was clasped in the waiting man's embrace. Longarm and Callahan dismounted as they reached the pair. Then they stood waiting until Meg broke away from her grandfather and turned to them.

"After all the times I've talked about Grandpa, I surely don't need to introduce you," she said. Then, turning back to her grandfather, she continued. "The big man on the left is Marshal Long, the one on the right is Marshal Callahan."

"Long," the old chief marshal said as he shook Longarm's extended hand. "You'd be the one they call Longarm. I've heard about you." Then he shook hands with Callahan. "And I recall you real good, Callahan, but I wasn't expecting to see you. Last I heard about you was that you'd turned in your badge."

"Billy Vail got me to pin it on again," Callahan replied. "But I don't aim to keep it on after this case is closed."

"Well, I've always heard that any case Longarm works gets closed sooner than later." Barrett smiled. "Now, from the way all three of you look, you've been doing some tall traveling. I'm not aiming to ask any questions right now. We'll hash things over after supper. By then, I expect this granddaughter of mine can find something that'll fit her better and be a tad more comfortable. Anyhow, we'll all go inside, because supper's going to be on the table in about half an hour."

"Looks to me like I owe you, Longarm," Barrett said. "And Callahan too."

"Now, you don't owe us nothing, and we ain't finished this case yet," Longarm said quickly. "It won't be closed till we've got Struthers and as many of his outlaw gang as we can run down."

"I didn't figure you had 'em corralled," Barrett said. "And if I hadn't sacked up my saddle a long time ago, I'd be riding with you when you set out after that bunch again."

Longarm, Callahan, and Meg were sitting with Barrett in the living room after supper. The old chief marshal had listened without interrupting to the two men as they'd sketched details of their encounter with the rustler gang. He'd also maintained a tight-lipped silence while hearing his granddaughter's greatly censored version of her capture and treatment at the hands of Struthers and his outlaw gang.

Now Barrett went on. "I can fill in the gaps as well as the next man. Maybe better'n most, because I've been there and seen it all too many times. If I've learned anything, it's that outlaws and renegades don't change their ways. What I'm thinking of what they done to my grandchild ain't fit to talk about."

"Don't worry about me, Grandpa," Meg said quickly. "I'm fine. All you've got to do is look at me to tell that."

"It ain't what I see or don't see that burns at me," he told her. "It's what I know about that outlaw gang."

"And I know more about those men than either one of you," Meg stated. Looking challengingly at Longarm and Callahan and her grandfather, she went on. "I've never doubted that you men would be going on after the renegades, and whether you think I'm fit to or not, I'm going with you."

"Now, hold on a minute," Longarm began. "If—"

"No ifs, ands, nor buts," she declared. "This is my home country just the same as it is Grandpa's, and I've got a real strong hunch that you'll find those men. When you do, I intend to be with you, and there's not anything you can say or do that'll stop me."

For a moment, neither Longarm nor Callahan nor Coy Barrett spoke. Before the silence grew too strained, Longarm flicked his eyes from Barrett to Meg. The old chief marshal finally nodded, an almost imperceptible inclination of his head. Then Longarm faced the old chief marshal again.

"I'd say you got the right to go also, Chief Marshal," he said. "And you'd be welcome as the flowers in May. So we'll start out soon as there's light enough to see by."

"Then let's get to bed," Barrett said. "And you better sleep good, because it might just be a while before you'll have another chance to."

Longarm was stretched out on the broad double bed in the small bedroom Meg had shown him to after the group broke up. As tired as his muscles were from their long journey after leaving the scene of the battle with the rustlers, sleep had eluded him so far. He shut his eyes again. He'd lost track of the number of times he'd tried to sleep since he'd shed his clothes and blown out the lamp that stood on the dresser opposite the bed.

This time Longarm's eyelids had been closed for only a few moments when the small metallic clicking of the doorknob started his hand toward the chair beside the bed, where he'd placed his Colt. In the instant before Longarm had realized that it was not merely unlikely, but unthinkable that he was in danger, the door had opened and a shadowy figure had slipped into his room. Then Meg's whisper reached him through the darkness.

"Longarm?" she whispered. "Are you awake?"

"As wide-eyed as I'll ever be. I reckon I'm too tired to let go and drop off to sleep."

"I've had the same trouble," Meg said as she closed the door behind her. "But that's because all I could think of was coming to be with you."

"Well, you know you're sure welcome," Longarm said. "But I sorta figured that after what those outlaws . . ."

"So did I," she said. "And I'm not ashamed to admit I was afraid that I'd never want a man to touch me again. Maybe it's just being back home, I don't know. But I'm aching right now to get on that bed with you, and . . ."

"Well, don't ache no more," Longarm told her. "Just come on over—"

Before Longarm could finish what he'd started to say, Meg was stretching out beside him. She had not taken time to remove the thin silken chemise she was wearing, and as Longarm rubbed a hand across her bulging breasts she began tugging at the slippery fabric to pull it up. The chemise yielded too slowly to please her. She twisted away from Longarm and sat up, tugging at the garment's fabric.

"Looks like you need a mite of help," Longarm said.

He fumbled his hand down Meg's body until he found a fold in its fabric, then slid his free hand under her back to lift her and assist her efforts. Between them they got the chemise above her head. Meg tugged and twisted her shoulders until the flimsy garment yielded. Then she tossed it to the floor and turned again to Longarm.

He'd reached a full erection now. Meg fondled his swollen shaft for only the moment required for Longarm to raise himself above her. Lifting her hips as she spread her thighs apart, Meg fumbled briefly as she placed him. Then she raised her hips and twisted from side to side as he thrust with a single, swift, forceful penetration that brought a gasp from her lips and started her body to quivering.

"Oh, yes!" she breathed. "Now drive, Longarm! Drive hard and fast and deep!"

Longarm was only too ready to oblige her. He began stroking, his full, swift penetrations bringing throaty sighs of pleasure from Meg's lips. The sighs became small gasps as

Longarm's thrusts continued. Then the sighs turned to cries as her body began shivering. The ripples flowed smoothly and rhythmically for only a few moments, for her hips soon started gyrating and jerking.

Longarm read her signs and began to thrust with even greater vigor while Meg was greeting his penetrations with ever-louder wails. Longarm bent to close her lips with his. Even as their tongues entwined, Meg's squirms became shudders that rippled through her frantically twisting body. The shudders reached a peak in growing waves until with a final sighing gasp, her squirming stopped abruptly.

Longarm kept driving for another moment or two, deep thrusts that triggered the climax he'd been witholding. As his own shudders died, be sagged and lowered himself gently to relax upon Meg's now-motionless body. They lay in silence for a while, and she was the first to break the hush that had claimed the room.

"You're a lot of man, Longarm," Meg said. She sighed contentedly. "And I hope you won't wait too long before proving it to me again."

"Oh, I'm just resting a minute," he assured her. "And sunup's quite a spell ahead. When you've got your wind back you just give a wiggle, and then I'll know it's time for me to start up again."

Chapter 15

"Now the way I look at it, there's two things we can do," Longarm told his companions. They'd stopped and re-formed into a compact group after splashing across the Blanco River at a firm sandy-bottomed stretch selected by Barrett. "We can circle around and have a try at picking up the tracks those outlaws made, or we can make a guess about where they ran to when they skedaddled away from the herd."

Coy Barrett said quickly, "If my opinion's worth anything, the first thing we'd better do is make sure we're still on their trail. Any other time than this one, I'd've bet they scattered, but right now I'd say they'll be sticking together."

"And I'd bet you're right, Coy," Longarm said.

"Now from everything you've told us, there was a pretty good-sized bunch of them," the old chief marshal stated. "How many of the gang were left after your fracas, Longarm?"

"That's real hard to figure," Longarm frowned. "All I can do is guess, but I'd say there was most likely six."

"I don't like to butt in, but I've got more reason than any of you for remembering," Meg said. "There were eight men, including their boss, that beastly Struthers."

"There weren't all that many left when me and Cal cut a shuck," Longarm said quickly. "We put at least two of 'em down, so if Struthers is still around, which I figure he might be, most likely there's still about six of 'em. We were so busy all the time that I wasn't much interested in counting noses."

"Or bodies," Callahan added. "My guess is there's not more than four of 'em left. Maybe five, with Struthers."

"Then we'll meet 'em on even terms," Coy Barrett said. "And now that we're going after them, we'll want to ride fast."

"And head which way?" Longarm asked.

"There's a bunch of little hills up ahead to the north of here," Barrett answered. "They're not big enough to be called mountains or have a name of their own. But it's the closest cover around, and in my day the outlaws used to hole up in 'em. I'd bet you any amount you'd care to put up that they still do."

"Then it appears like we're in business," Longarm said. "You show us the way, Chief Marshal. There ain't none of us that don't have a right good reason for nabbing what's left of that outfit, so the sooner we run 'em down, the better."

Coy Barrett reined in when the level prairie over which they'd been riding started to slope gently upward, and the others followed his example. The sun hung midway in the eastern sky now, and the occasional breezes that had been blowing over the generally level prairie no longer brought them a passing breath of cool air. The heat haze was beginning to form above the drying prairie grass, and ahead of them the once-clear air had started to shimmer, veiling the landscape which had been so clearly visible when they'd set out.

Barrett waved toward the horizon as he said, "You can't see too much about it this far away, but that dark high blob that breaks the prairie right ahead of us is the hills I was telling you about."

"I sure can't make much out of 'em from here," Longarm said. "But I been watching the lay of the land, and I'd say that a bunch of rustlers looking for a close-by place to hole up would just about be bound to head for any hill they could find."

"That's the way it used to be, and I don't imagine it's changed much," Barrett said. "Days past, I've seen more'n one rustler gang that had run for cover up in that stand of hills come out of 'em feet-first."

"And I'd bet you've been over just about every inch of ground that's in 'em during the time you were chief marshal," Longarm suggested.

"You'd win that bet hands-down," Barrett replied. "I don't guess I've forgotten where the caves and rock splits and other kinds of hidey-holes are."

"How many ways do you figure there is to get to the top?"

"That's easy," Barrett told him. "There's just one good trail going up or down, and once you get on top it opens up into a sort of Y. All we'll have to do is split up at the forks and prowl around a little bit to flush out that bunch of rascals."

"Then let's get moving," Longarm said. He continued to scan the expanse of level prairie that stretched between them and the hills. "There sure ain't no cover between us and it, so about all we can do is put you in the lead and follow wherever you take us."

"I've done it enough before so this one more time won't faze me a bit." Barrett grinned, then suddenly his face grew

161

sober. He gestured for Longarm to step away from the group for a moment, and when they'd moved apart from the others the old man said, "All I'm worried about is that granddaughter of mine getting hurt. You think you could talk her into staying behind?"

Longarm shook his head slowly as he answered. "Not any more'n you could. All I can see to do is put her in the back of the bunch and let her ride right along."

"I know you're right, so I won't waste time arguing," the old marshal said. "We'll start then. The sooner we get on top of those hills, the closer we'll be to finishing what the damned outlaws started."

A bit less than an hour of steady progress had taken Longarm and the impromptu posse to the base of the little twin hillocks that had been their goal. They'd wasted no time looking for tracks, but had ridden on a straight line and covered the ground quickly. Then, at Coy Barrett's suggestion, they'd ridden a bit more than halfway to the lower of the two crests of the rising hills. Now Barrett pulled up and motioned for the others to come to him.

"I just learned one way to scout around in country like this," he told them. "And that's to spread out wide as we can without any of us losing sight of the rest."

"You mean riding in line?" Longarm asked.

Barrett nodded. "We'll spread here, and start up the hills. Longarm, you take one end. Cal, you take the other one. Margaret, you stay between me and Longarm. Try to keep about a quarter of a mile apart and go up straight."

"How high will we go?" Meg asked.

"Halfway, maybe a bit more," Barrett replied. "And round as the tops of these hills are, we won't be all that much apart when we get close to the top. If we don't find 'em the first sweep, we'll go partway around this hill, and look for 'em going downwards. Then if we still haven't found 'em, we'll go on to the twin hill and do the same thing."

Almost before the old chief marshal had finished outlining their search strategy, the group was dividing. Within a few moments they were in place and starting their mounts up the hill's steep sides. In his position at one end of the sweep-line Longarm could see Meg, but Barrett was visible only intermittently, and Callahan was completely hidden from his view.

Meg had already advanced almost a quarter of a mile up the slope before Longarm toed his mount to a faster pace in order to keep abreast of her. After he'd gotten to a stretch of reasonably clear ground ahead where he could rein his horse up-slope again, he lost sight of her only occasionally, at points where a solitary high rock outcrop came between them.

They crossed the wide stretch of almost-smooth terrain, and were approaching an area where wide vertical crevasses yawned close together in the broken ground when the first shot rang out. A puff of dust spurted up a few inches from the forefeet of Margaret's horse. Longarm was carrying his rifle across his thighs. Before the echoes of the shot had died away he was holding the weapon ready to shoulder it, scanning the rocky terrain ahead, looking for a target.

He found one within a few seconds, a paper-thin trail of gunsmoke rising from a rock outcrop ahead, barely visible in the clear morning air. Holding his Winchester across his chest, ready to raise its muzzle and fire, Longarm waited. His wait was not a long one. The barrel of a rifle appeared above a long high rock ledge in front of him. Longarm had the butt of his own rifle pulled into his shoulder now. He waited until the head and shoulders of the man holding the weapon broke the jagged skyline, then took quick aim and triggered off a shot.

He saw the rifleman jerk with the impact of his bullet. The outlaw had not yet leveled his rifle when another shot rang out from Meg's rifle. Again Longarm saw the outlaw's body jerk as the bullet took him, but he did not hold his own fire. He triggered another shot and the outlaw's body started sagging, then slid down and was lost to sight.

Distant gunshots had already started sounding from the area where Coy Barrett and Cal Callahan had started up the steep slope. Longarm glanced in the direction of the shots, and now he could see Meg clearly where she'd appeared from behind one of the many rock outcrops that rose on the striated hillside. She waved to him, and he returned the wave, then she beckoned for him to join her.

Longarm shook his head just as another scattering of rifle fire crackled from beyond them, in the area where Barrett and Callahan were mounting the slope. Meg gestured again toward the direction from which the shots were coming. Longarm shook his head and waved toward the up-slanting ground that still rose ahead of them. Meg waited for a moment, then nodded and re-started her horse up the slope, keeping abreast of Longarm.

By this time the distant gunfire had faded to an occasional shot. Now Longarm decided to edge toward Meg. He toed his horse once more, and did not rein in until he was within a dozen yards of her. Meg changed her course and started to approach him, but he shook his head and gestured toward the narrowing strip of the up-slope that still remained in front of them.

"I'd lay dollars to doughnuts there's an outlaw or two waiting in back of that hump ahead," he called. "And we better be ready if I'm right, because them scoundrels have had plenty of time to pick out the best places to snipe at us from."

Meg nodded and reined aside to change her course just as a rifle spat from the shelter of a high rock shelf ahead of them. The slug kicked up dust and pebbles just short of

Longarm's horse, and before the dust raised by the bullet had settled Longarm was swiveling in his saddle, bringing up his rifle.

At almost point-blank range ahead of them the head and shoulders of one of the outlaws rose, his rifle already raised, coming down to aim at Margaret. Longarm saw instantly that he had no time to shoulder the Winchester. Cradling it in his bent elbow, his finger already seeking the trigger, he snap-shot at the half-visible target the outlaw presented. The man's body jerked as the rifle slug took him in the chest. Then he toppled backward while his rifle clattered to the ground.

"That was too close for comfort," Meg called to Longarm. "I won't forget it for a long time!"

"You'd best keep it in mind right now," Longarm cautioned her. Before he'd finished speaking a chatter of distant shots reached their ears. "Sounds like your granddad and Callahan's got a few of them outlaws corralled."

"And not very far from here either!" she said.

"It ain't likely there's any more of 'em right up ahead of us," Longarm declared. "We're too close to the top here. Let's slant over and see if them fellows could use a little help."

With one accord they reined around the sloping surface of the hilltop and started in the direction of the shots. As they moved forward the firing slackened and then died away. The first indication that they were nearing the area where the shots had sounded was the sprawled body of one of the outlaws, his sightless eyes gazing upward, his rifle lying across his thighs.

"Looks like your granddad and Callahan have been doing a little shooting themselves," Longarm commented. "If I ain't wrong, there's just maybe three or four more of the renegades left, and that'll level out the odds a lot."

"Do you think we can find the rest of them?" Meg asked. "Or will they take off and start running away?"

"Well, now, they're likely to do most anything," Longarm told her. "But we're in the catbird seat now. Once the renegades break cover and start running, we'll be so close to 'em that picking them off's going to be easy as catching fish outa a rain barrel."

Longarm suddenly leaned toward Meg, pulling her out of her saddle and dropping with her to the ground as a rifle barked from a cluster of big boulders ahead of them and its slug whistled over the backs of their horses.

"Lucky I saw that rifle muzzle up ahead in time," Longarm commented as he slid two fresh shells into the loading port of his Winchester. Then, as though he and Meg were exchanging pleasantries in a street, he went on. "What I'd begun to say was we'll be all right if we just mind our p's and q's. Now, you stay right here a minute."

"Where are you going?"

"Why, I'm aiming to circle around to someplace where I can lay my sights on that fellow that just took a shot at us. You let off a round or two at him soon as I get going. It don't make no never-mind whether you can see him or not."

"But, Longarm, if you—"

"Never mind ifs, ands, or buts," he admonished her. "Just keep him thinking both of us are still here."

Before Meg could protest further, Longarm was bellycrawling around the edge of the sheltering boulder. Another distant shot echoed as he was disappearing, and a third sounded after he'd started toward the hidden rustler.

Longarm had barely started up the slope ahead when the outlaw who had been firing at them stood up, his rifle shouldered. Longarm had been holding his rifle by the throat of its stock; it took no time at all for him to get the weapon's butt on his shoulder. His shot was echoed by the bark of

Meg's weapon, the two reports blending into one.

Before their echoes had died away the outlaw was pitching forward, his rifle dropping from lifeless hands. Then Meg called from her sheltered position, "We got him, Longarm!"

"Sure looks thataway," he agreed. "Now all we got to do is dig out the rest."

In the distance a rattle of gunfire sounded, a dozen or more shots in quick succession. A few minutes of silence followed, then Coy Barrett's voice reached them.

"Meg! Longarm! Come on back, unless you see any more outlaws! I heard you shooting, and I've been tallying the bunch we just busted up, so I'd say we've wiped the slate clean!"

"I'd say he's right," Longarm commented.

"Yes, Grandpa usually is," Meg agreed. "And I suppose that means you'll be moving on?"

"Well, there's lots of other outlaws in lots of other places," Longarm replied. "You put 'em all together, they add up to a pretty big stack."

"But it'll be late by the time we get back."

"Now, don't go fretting so soon," Longarm told her. "Me and Cal ain't in all that much of a hurry. We'll stay the night, and maybe another one while we figure where we're going next."

"Then, I won't worry about tonight." Meg smiled.

"Don't," Longarm said. "We had a long day, and I can't think of no better reason for us to go to bed early and stay there till it's way past daylight tomorrow."

Watch for

LONGARM AND THE DOUBLE EAGLES

166th in the bold LONGARM series from Jove

Coming in October!

SPECIAL PREVIEW!

Award-winning author Bill Gulick presents his epic
trilogy of the American West, the magnificent story of
two brothers, Indian and white man, bound by blood
and divided by destiny . . .

Northwest Destiny

This classic saga includes *Distant Trails, Gathering
Storm,* and *River's End.*

*Following is a special excerpt from Volume One,
DISTANT TRAILS—available from Jove books . . .*

For the last hundred yards of the stalk, neither man had spoken—not even in whispers—but communicated by signs as they always did when hunting meat to fill hungry bellies. Two steps ahead, George Drewyer, the man recognized to be the best hunter in the Lewis and Clark party, sank down on his right knee, froze, and peered intently through the glistening wet bushes and dangling evergreen tree limbs toward the animal grazing in the clearing. Identifying it, he turned, using his hands swiftly and graphically to tell the younger, less experienced hunter, Matt Crane, the nature of the animal he had seen and how he meant to approach and kill it.

Not a deer, his hands said. Not an elk. Just a stray Indian horse—with no Indians in sight. He'd move up on it from downwind, his hands said, until he got into sure-kill range, then he'd put a ball from his long rifle into its head. What he expected Matt to do was follow a couple of steps behind and a few feet off to the right, stopping when he stopped, aiming when he aimed, but firing only if the actions of the horse clearly showed that Drewyer's ball had missed.

Matt signed that he understood. Turning back toward the clearing, George Drewyer began his final stalk.

Underfoot, the leaf mold and fallen pine needles formed a yielding carpet beneath the scattered clumps of bushes and thick stands of pines, which here on the western slope of the Bitter Root Mountains were broader in girth and taller than the skinny lodgepole and larch found on the higher reaches of the Lolo Trail. Half a day's travel behind, the other thirty-two members of the party still were struggling in foot-deep snow over slick rocks, steep slides, and tangles of down timber treacherous as logjams, as they sought the headwaters of the Columbia and the final segment of their journey to the Pacific Ocean.

It had been four days since the men had eaten meat, Matt knew, being forced to sustain themselves on the detested army ration called "portable soup," a grayish brown jelly that looked like a mixture of pulverized wood duff and dried dung, tasted like iron filings, and even when flavored with meat drippings and dissolved in hot water satisfied the belly no more than a swallow of air. Nor had the last solid food been much, for the foal butchered at Colt-Killed Creek had been dropped by its dam only a few months ago; though its meat was tender enough, most of its growth had gone into muscle and bone, its immature carcass making skimpy portions when distributed among such a large party of famished men.

With September only half gone, winter had already come to the seven-thousand-foot-high backbone of the continent a week's travel behind. All the game that the old Shoshone guide, Toby, had told them usually was to be found in the high meadows at this time of year had moved down to lower levels. Desperate for food, Captain William Clark had sent George Drewyer and Matt Crane scouting ahead for meat, judging that two men traveling afoot and unencumbered would stand a much better chance of finding game than the main party with its thirty-odd men and twenty-nine heavily laden horses. As he usually did, Drewyer had found game of a sort, weighed the risk of rousing the hostility of its Indian owner against the need of the party for food, and decided that hunger recognized no property rights.

In the drizzling cold rain, the coat of the grazing horse glistened like polished metal. It would be around four years old, Matt guessed, a brown and white paint, well muscled, sleek, alert. If this were a typical Nez Perce horse, he could well believe what the Shoshone chief, Cameahwait, had told Captain Clark—that the finest horses to be found in this part of the country were those raised by the Shoshones' mortal enemies, the Nez Perces. Viewing such a handsome animal cropping bluegrass on a Missouri hillside eighteen months ago, Matt Crane would have itched to rope, saddle, and ride it, testing its speed, wind, and spirit. Now all he itched to do was kill and eat it.

Twenty paces away from the horse, which still was grazing placidly, George Drewyer stopped, knelt behind a fallen tree, soundlessly rested the barrel of his long rifle on its trunk, and took careful aim. Two steps to his right, Matt Crane did the same. After what seemed an agonizingly long period of time, during which Matt held his breath, Drewyer's rifle barked. Without movement or sound, the paint horse sank to the ground, dead—Matt was sure—before its body touched the sodden earth.

"Watch it!" Drewyer murmured, swiftly reversing his rifle, swabbing out its barrel with the ramrod, expertly reloading it with patched and greased lead ball, wiping flint and firing hammer clean, then opening the pan and pouring in a carefully measured charge while he protected it from the drizzle with the tree trunk and his body.

Keeping his own rifle sighted on the fallen horse, Matt held his position without moving or speaking, as George Drewyer had taught him to do, until the swarthy, dark-eyed hunter had reloaded his weapon and risen to one knee. Peering first at the still animal, then moving his searching gaze around the clearing, Drewyer tested the immediate environment with all his senses—sight, sound, smell, and his innate hunter's instinct—for a full minute before he at last nodded in satisfaction.

"A bunch-quitter, likely. Least there's no herd nor herders around. Think you can skin it, preacher boy?"

"Sure. You want it quartered, with the innards saved in the hide?"

"Just like we'd do with an elk. Save everything but the hoofs and whinny. Get at it, while I snoop around for Injun sign. The Nez Perces will be friendly, the captains say, but I'd as soon not meet the Injun that owned that horse till its head and hide are out of sight."

While George Drewyer circled the clearing and prowled through the timber beyond, Matt Crane went to the dead horse, unsheathed his butcher knife, skillfully made the cuts needed to strip off the hide, and gutted and dissected the animal. Returning from his scout, Drewyer hunkered down beside him, quickly boned out as large a packet of choice cuts as he could conveniently carry, wrapped them in a piece of hide, and loaded the still-warm meat into the empty canvas backpack he had brought along for that purpose.

"It ain't likely the men'll get this far by dark," he said, "so I'll take 'em a taste to ease their bellies for the night. Can you make out alone till tomorrow noon?"

"Yes."

"From what I seen, the timber thins out a mile or so ahead. Seems to be a kind of open, marshy prairie beyond, which is where the Nez Perces come this time of year to dig roots,

Toby says. Drag the head and hide back in the bushes out of sight. Cut the meat up into pieces you can spit and broil, then build a fire and start it cooking. If the smoke and smell brings Injun company, give 'em the peace sign, invite 'em to sit and eat, and tell 'em a big party of white men will be coming down the trail tomorrow. You got all that, preacher boy?"

"Yes."

"Good. Give me a hand with this pack and I'll be on my way." Slipping his arms through the straps and securing the pad that transferred a portion of the weight to his forehead, Drewyer got to his feet while Matt Crane eased the load. Grinning, Drewyer squeezed his shoulder. "Remind me to quit calling you preacher boy, will you, Matt? You've learned a lot since you left home."

"I've had a good teacher."

"That you have! Take care."

Left alone in the whispering silence of the forest and the cold, mist-like rain, Matt Crane dragged the severed head and hide into a clump of nearby bushes. Taking his hatchet, he searched for and found enough resinous wood, bark, and dry duff to catch the spark from his flint and steel. As the fire grew in the narrow trench he had dug for it, he cut forked sticks, placed pieces of green aspen limbs horizontally across them, sliced the meat into strips, and started it to broiling. The smell of juice dripping into the fire made his belly churn with hunger, tempting him to do what Touissant Charbonneau, the party's French-Canadian interpreter, did when fresh-killed game was brought into camp—seize a hunk and gobble it down hot, raw, and bloody. But he did not, preferring to endure the piercing hunger pangs just a little longer in exchange for the greater pleasure of savoring his first bite of well-cooked meat.

Cutting more wood for the fire, he hoped George Drewyer would stop calling him "preacher boy." Since at twenty he was one of the youngest members of the party and his father, the Reverend Peter Crane, was a Presbyterian minister in St. Louis, it had been natural enough for the older men to call him "the preacher's boy" at first. Among a less disciplined band, he would have been forced to endure a good deal of hoorawing and would have been the butt of many practical jokes. But the no-nonsense military leadership of the two captains put strict limits on that sort of thing.

Why Drewyer—who'd been raised a Catholic, could barely read and write, and had no peer as an outdoorsman— should have made Matt his protégé, Matt himself could not guess. Maybe because he was malleable, did what he was told to do, and never backed off from hard work. Maybe because he listened more than he talked. Or maybe because he was having the adventure of his life and showed it. Whatever the reason, their relationship was good. It would be even better, Matt mused, if Drewyer would drop the "preacher boy" thing and simply call him by name.

While butchering the horse, Matt noticed that it had been gelded as a colt. According to George Drewyer, the Nez Perces were one of the few Western Indian tribes that practiced selective breeding, thus the high quality of their horses. From the way Chief Cameahwait had acted, a state of war existed between the Shoshones and the Nez Perces, so the first contact between the Lewis and Clark party— which had passed through Shoshone country—and the Nez Perces was going to be fraught with danger. Aware of the fact that he might make the first contact, Matt Crane felt both uneasy and proud. Leaving him alone in this area showed the confidence Drewyer had in him. But his aloneness made him feel a little spooky.

With the afternoon only half gone and nothing to do but tend the fire, Matt stashed his blanket roll under a tree out of the wet, picked up his rifle, and curiously studied the surrounding forest. There was no discernible wind, but vagrant currents of air stirred, bringing to his nostrils the smell of wood smoke, of crushed pine needles, of damp leaf mold, of burnt black powder. As he moved across the clearing toward a three-foot-wide stream gurgling down the slope, he scowled, suddenly realizing that the burnt black powder smell could not have lingered behind this long. Nor would it have gotten stronger, as this smell was doing the nearer he came to the stream. Now he identified it beyond question.

Sulfur! There must be a mineral-impregnated hot spring nearby, similar to the hot springs near Traveler's Rest at the eastern foot of Lolo Pass, where the cold, weary members of the party had eased their aches and pains in warm, soothing pools. What he wouldn't give for a hot bath right now!

At the edge of the stream, he knelt, dipping his hand into the water. It was warm. Cupping his palm, he tasted it, finding it strongly sulfurous. If this were like the stream on the other side of the mountains, he mused, there would be one or more scalding, heavily impregnated springs issuing from old volcanic rocks higher up the slope, their waters diluted by colder side rivulets joining the main stream, making it simply a matter of exploration to find water temperature and a chemical content best suited to the needs of a cold, tired body. The prospect intrigued him.

Visually checking the meat broiling over the fire, he judged it could do without tending for an hour or so. Thick though the forest cover was along the sides of the stream, he would run no risk of getting lost, for following the stream downhill would bring him back to the clearing. Time enough then to cut limbs for a lean-to and rig a shelter for the night.

Sometimes wading in the increasingly warm waters of the stream, sometimes on its bush-bordered bank, he followed its windings uphill for half a mile before he found what he was looking for: a pool ten feet long and half as wide, eroded in smooth basalt, ranging in depth from one to four feet. Testing the temperature of its water, he found it just right—hot but not unbearably so, the sulfur smell strong but not unpleasant. Leaning his rifle against a tree trunk, he took off his limp, shapeless red felt hat, pulled his thin moccasins off his bruised and swollen feet, waded into the pool, and gasped with sensual pleasure as the heat of the water spread upward.

Since his fringed buckskin jacket and woolen trousers already were soaking wet from the cold rain, he kept them on as he first sank to a sitting position, then stretched out full length on his back, with only his head above water. After a time, he roused himself long enough to strip the jacket off over his head and pull the trousers down over his ankles. Tossing them into a clump of bushes near his rifle, hat, and moccasins, he lay back in the soothing water, naked, warm, and comfortable for the first time since Traveler's Rest.

Drowsily, his eyes closed. He slept . . .

The sound that awakened him some time later could have been made by a deer moving down to drink from the pool just upstream from where he lay. It could have been made by a beaver searching for a choice willow sapling to cut down. It could have been made by a bobcat, a bear, or a cougar. But as consciousness returned to him, as he heard the sound and attempted to identify it, his intelligence rejected each possibility that occurred to him the moment it crossed his mind—for one lucid reason.

Animals did not sing. And whatever this intruder into his state of tranquility might be, it was singing.

Though the words were not recognizable, they had an Indian sound, unmistakably conveying the message that the singer was at peace with the world, not self-conscious, and about to indulge in a very enjoyable act. Turning over on his belly, Matt crawled to the upper end of the pool, peering through the screening bushes in the direction from which the singing sound was coming. The light was poor. Even so, it was good enough for him to make out the figure of a girl, standing in profile not ten feet away, reaching down to the hem of her buckskin skirt, lifting it, and pulling it up over her head.

As she tossed the garment aside, she turned, momentarily facing him. His first thought was *My God, she's beautiful!* His second: *She's naked!* His third: *How can I get away from here without being seen?*

That she was not aware of his presence was made clear enough by the fact that she still was crooning her bath-taking song, her gaze intent on her footing as she stepped gingerly into a pool just a few yards upstream from the one in which he lay. Though he had stopped breathing for fear she would hear the sound, he could not justify leaving his eyes open for fear she would hear the lids closing. Morally wrong though he knew it was to stare at her, he could not even blink or look away.

She would be around sixteen years old, he judged, her skin light copper in color, her mouth wide and generous, with dimples indenting both cheeks. Her breasts were full but not heavy; her waist was slim, her stomach softly rounded, her hips beginning to broaden with maturity, her legs long and graceful. Watching her sink slowly into the water until only the tips of her breasts and her head were exposed, Matt felt no guilt for continuing to stare at her. Instead he mused, *So that's what a naked woman looks like! Why should I be ashamed to admire such beauty?*

He began breathing again, careful to make no sound. Since the two pools were no more than a dozen feet apart, separated by a thin screen of bushes and a short length of stream, which here made only a faint gurgling noise, he knew that getting out of the water, retrieving his clothes and rifle, and then withdrawing from the vicinity without revealing his presence would require utmost caution. But the attempt must be made, for if one young Indian woman knew of this bathing spot, others must know of it, too, and in all likelihood soon would be coming here to join her.

He could well imagine his treatment at their hands, if found. Time and again recently the two captains had warned members of the party that Western Indians such as the Shoshones, Flatheads, and Nez Perces had a far higher standard of morality than did the Mandans, with whom the party had wintered, who would gladly sell the favor of wives and daughters for a handful of beads, a piece of bright cloth, or a cheap trade knife, and cheerfully provide shelter and bed for the act.

Moving with infinite care, he half floated, half crawled to the lower right-hand edge of the pool, where he had left his rifle and clothes. The Indian girl still was singing. The bank was steep and slick. Standing up, he took hold of a sturdy-feeling, thumb-thick sapling rooted near the edge of the bank, cautiously tested it, and judged it secure. Pulling himself out of the pool, he started to take a step, slipped, and tried to save himself by grabbing the sapling with both hands.

The full weight of his body proved too much for its root system. Torn out of the wet earth, it no longer supported him. As he fell backward into the pool, he gave an involuntary cry of disgust.

"Oh, shit!"

Underwater, his mouth, nose, and eyes filled as he struggled to turn over and regain his footing. When he did so, he immediately became aware of the fact that the girl had stopped singing. Choking, coughing up water, half-blinded, and completely disoriented, he floundered out of the pool toward where he thought his clothes and rifle were. Seeing a garment draped over a bush, he grabbed it, realized it was not his, hastily turned away, and blundered squarely into a wet, naked body.

To save themselves from falling, both he and the Indian girl clung to each other momentarily. She began screaming. Hastily he let her go. Still screaming and staring at him with terror-stricken eyes, she snatched her dress off the bush and held it so that it covered her. Finding his own clothes, he held them in front of his body, trying to calm the girl by making the sign for "friend," "white man," and "peace," while urgently saying:

"*Ta-ba-bone,* you understand? *Suyapo!* I went to sleep, you see, and had no idea you were around . . ."

Suddenly her screaming stopped. Not because of his words or hand signs, Matt feared, but because of the appearance of an Indian man who had pushed through the bushes and now stood beside her. He was dressed in beaded, fringed buckskins, was stocky, slightly bowlegged, a few inches shorter than Matt but more muscular and heavier, a man in his middle twenties, with high cheekbones and a firm jawline. He shot a guttural question at the girl, to which she replied in a rapid babble of words. His dark brown eyes blazed with anger. Drawing a glittering knife out of its sheath, he motioned the girl to step aside, and moved toward Matt menacingly.

Backing away, Matt thought frantically, *Captain Clark is not going to like this at all. And if that Indian does what it looks like he means to do with that knife, I'm not going to like it, either . . .*